WANDER

A RUCKSACK UNIVERSE NOVEL

ANTHONY ST. CLAIR

RUCKSACK PRESS

"There is a road that is flat, broad, and straight. It can take you all over Ireland, and it is a straight line to London. Yet it is a road that none dare travel. I tried once to set foot upon it. When I did, the sense of grief and sadness, the only vibrant thing amidst all the death there, made me resolve to never go near the Black Road again."

—Guru Deep, *Ireland Through the Third Eye*

PART I

$$1$$

HAPPY BIRTHDAY

"How did you know it was my birthday?" asked Wander.

Sitting behind his desk at the front of the hostel, Rashid, the elderly proprietor, looked up from his computer and smiled. "Your passport," he replied. "Twenty. A wonderful year. A time when many things may change."

Wander smiled back. The past five years had been nothing but a time of change. Six months wandering South America, and another two years wandering Africa. Seven months in Ireland, a year in Russia. Indonesia in the morning, Australia at night. With no family or friends, birthdays were just another day to check off the calendar. Now, at the southwestern coast of Morocco, the warm waters of the eastern Atlantic brought salt in on the breeze. Maybe a birthday could be something to look forward to after all.

Wander leaned forward. "So, what should I do on my birthday?"

"Ahh, now that is a good question." Rashid sat back in his chair. "Check your email and all those social thingies, then come back. I will tell you then."

Wander sat at the hostel's computer. In the monitor's reflection, dim and faint, as if staring out from another world, was a face that could be any face—male or female, young or old—with any shape, any skin shade, any hairstyle, anything whatsoever. The face of any traveler who has ever hit the road from any place that marked their first step. Wander had an anyoneness, an anywhereness that made Wander everyone in particular. An identity of all possibilities, as if the universe had split into infinite multiverses and anyone could set off on Wander's journey.

Logging on, Wander wondered how many other people in the world had access to the internet but didn't have a Facespace account. Or a Twitlinkpinstatoob+. Opening the daypack, Wander took out a small flip phone. A traveler on a nearby couch looked up from her bright-screened, too-big-for-the-hand Apsamgoo iGalixel and smirked.

"Trust me." Wander's not-too-high, not-too-low voice competed with the beeps and boops coming from the traveler's phone. "Last thing I need is a data plan or unlimited messaging."

The traveler shrugged. Instead of looking back at her phone, she stared at Wander. A wavy, wobbly silence passed between the two travelers. Wander could see the question forming in the traveler's eyes. Are you a girl or a guy? A man or a woman?

Wander grinned and leaned forward, smoldering eyes narrow. "You'll never know."

The traveler's gaze darted back down to her phone. Wander chuckled and returned to the computer.

It had been a while since Wander had checked email—somewhere between Thailand and Morocco, but that time had been such a whirlwind that Wander could hardly remember it. Not that it mattered.

Zero messages.

Not that there was anyone who would be emailing. Or throwing a surprise party. Or sending a card.

When your only friends were your backpack and the stretch of road currently under your feet, you learned not to make a big deal out of birthdays.

At twenty years old, though, Wander couldn't help but hope for just one note from a friend, one sign of acknowledgment that Wander was still in the world. It wasn't that Wander didn't meet anyone. There were plenty of people Wander had connected with over the years. Random wanderings together in a new city. Dorm-mates in a hostel room. That traveler in Galway, Ireland. When they met, Wander wondered what else could have happened between them. They'd exchanged info... that last touch of hand on hand had been so hard to let go of... but now, on Wander's birthday... nothing. Wander looked away. The screen must be too bright. Of course that's why Wander's eyes hurt all of a sudden.

There was always Paithoon in Chiang Mai too. Then again, not hearing from Paithoon was maybe a good thing.

With a sigh and a shrug, Wander logged off email, then the computer. Moving to the little table at the window of the hostel's common room, Wander stared at the ocean. Blue rising. White-caps cresting, then falling. The dry air mingled with the sea spray, suffusing everything with the taste and scent of salt. The few days Wander had been here had been calm, refreshing—badly needed, especially after all that had happened in Thailand with Paithoon.

The memories stirred, the remembered dreams, the remembered past, hard won from five years of traveling and weeks of frustration and sleeplessness, trying to uncover a personal forgotten history. Wander had been more than ready to move on. The southwestern coast of Morocco, staring out over the Atlantic, was as good as anywhere else, but those final moments in Chiang Mai still clung to Wander's mind. A storm had come, a storm had passed, and now Wander was enjoying the calm. At least, it felt like calm. But Wander knew a question cast a shadow even over the bright Moroccan morning: Was the storm truly over, or was this the quiet eye—to be followed by more storm?

A tap on the shoulder made Wander turn.

With a smile, Rashid held out a large envelope, bigger than a regular sheet of paper.

"What's this?" asked Wander.

Rashid shrugged and set it down. "Today's mail." He left to answer the phone.

The side Wander saw was blank. Turning it over, Wander saw that there was no return address—not even a mailing address. Just "Wander," written in a fine script with immaculate—and familiar —handwriting.

Wander opened the envelope and gasped.

The stiff thick sheet inside was like Wander's favorite painting, called *The Wanderer in the Fog*. In that painting, the figure held a walking stick, wore a black tailcoat, and stared out over mountains and valleys. What was before Wander, though, was similar yet different.

Running a fingertip over the rough and smooth textures of the art, Wander had no doubt this was an original painting. A narrow finger of rock jutted out from the edge of a rocky cliff. On it, a figure stood before a sheer drop to a white-capped, gray-blue sea below. At the far edge of the sea, Wander could just make out a thin line, as if a new world lay just beyond. Despite the blue sky, shadows obscured the figure so much that Wander could not tell if it was a woman or a man. The black rock of the cliff didn't look like it was in shadow, though. It looked like it had been burned and charred. Below the cliff, a strange, shadowy light seemed to glow upward from somewhere unseen, somewhere down the cliff toward the sea. It enhanced an overarching conflict, as if the painting were caught between darkness and light. Calm seas had grown teeth, whipped into a growing frenzy as a storm blew in.

The Wanderer in the Fog showed only one figure. So too did this similar painting—except the figure was in the foreground, at the left bottom corner.

Gloved in black leather, a left hand reached out toward the wanderer at the edge of the world.

Heart pounding, Wander turned the painting over and read:

No matter where you wander,
May you always find a
Happy Birthday

The Thai madwoman had signed her name. Wander smiled and let out a chuckle. It made no sense that Paithoon's painting had gotten from Chiang Mai to this hostel in Morocco, but if anyone could have managed it, it would be her.

Beneath the message was a P.S.:

I dreamed recently, and at the last moment of the dream, this is what I saw. I don't know how I knew it, and I don't know where this is, but I knew this was you.

Wander stared at the calm seas outside the hostel's window. The madwoman had to be wrong... but Wander knew better. Trembling a little, Wander tucked the painting back into the envelope.

"Happy birthday," said the traveler sitting nearby, with a nod toward the card. "I couldn't help but see."

Wander shrugged. "I'm glad someone noticed."

The sunlight coming through the window was warm, bright but soft. Wander had savored every moment so far, every bite of breakfast, every sensation, the touch of water on hands, the scent of tea. But this painting changed everything. A shadow hung over the sunny morning. Wander looked at the card again. A birthday could be a momentous day. A day in which someone could make a decision that just might change everything.

Wander considered going back to the dorm room and putting the card in the big pack there, but decided against it. The card was a memento, a reminder of what Paithoon had helped Wander learn, there in Thailand, those lonely, hard weeks ago. The daypack always went with Wander—and so would the card.

Wander unzipped the daypack and put the card inside. After

all these years, the pack reminded Wander of a dog, though by now it was an old dog. It was the one thing Wander still had from then, from there, when as a teenager Wander had been left with nothing and so had left with nothing. Except for the backpack. The one constant in Wander's life for the last five years.

With a sigh, Wander went back to the front desk. "So, what did you decide this here traveler should do today?"

Rashid cocked his bushy eyebrows. On a small piece of paper, he drew a map. He said nothing, only occasionally looked out the window, as if gauging something, checking something. Whenever he did, when he looked back the smile would be gone from his eyes, as if it had been taken by whatever he was looking for.

Or maybe he just wasn't looking forward to cleaning up the puke in the upstairs bathroom.

Accepting the map with a thanks, Wander started to walk away.

"Wait," said Rashid. "What you got in the mail. Was it good news?"

Wander shrugged. "You tell me." Reaching into the daypack, Wander handed him the painting.

Rashid looked at it, saying nothing, just staring and staring. He read the back. Then, at last, he looked at Wander.

"Well, this is interesting," he said. "I indeed gave you one option. But if you want, you could go here instead."

2

CLIFF

Rashid led the way.

"This is really nice of you," said Wander.

He shrugged. "A walk sounds far better than the alternative," he replied. "I knew that group would party too much. I'm in no hurry to clean up the bathroom."

They walked along the sand. The morning tide teased their bare toes. Ahead, a promontory rose from the beach, tall and rocky, but the rock was pale, not at all like the blackened rock in the painting. Soon they were walking up a narrow path, from the back of the promontory. For much of the walk, Wander could only hear the sea, not see it.

"There used to be a hill on top of this," said Rashid. "With a cave inside. But many thousands of years ago, the hill exploded and was no more."

"What happened?"

"No one knows," said Rashid. "There is no explanation here that anyone has ever found. But there are stories. Myths and legends. My favorite is one about an ancient hero and a villain whose pain would have brought about the end of all things."

"There are always stories. Aren't stories how we paper over the gaps of what we don't know?"

The proprietor grinned. "I like to think that stories create the bridges leading us from what we already know to what we don't know yet."

They came to the top, and Wander whistled.

The rock here was dark—blackened, as if it had been burned and charred.

"Just as there can be many fish swimming in the same ocean," said Rashid, "it is said that this is but one world in a sea of many. And some believe that many thousands of years ago, something happened in a world that, shall we say, is a neighbor of ours. Whatever happened there—on this spot but in that world—was so powerful that its effects were felt not just there, but here and perhaps in other worlds too."

"So you're saying some sort of explosion in another place blew up a hill here?"

The proprietor nodded.

"It's definitely a great story," said Wander.

"Sometimes," said the proprietor, "a great story is all you need."

At the edge of the promontory, looking out over the crashing sea, a small outcropping stretched away from the main rock.

The proprietor nodded toward the outcropping. "Do you want to stand there? It will look just like the painting."

"I know it must be me in the painting, but it's hard to imagine why I would be standing at the edge of a cliff," Wander tried to keep a level voice. "I... I hate heights."

"I will be near. Trust yourself. You won't fall."

"I trust myself. It's gravity that I have a problem with."

"It is your birthday," said Rashid. "Whatever you believe, whatever you think, the painting came to you, here, on your birthday. It must be the same place. You owe it to yourself. A birthday is a time of great change—and great change begins by facing great fear."

Wander sighed. "All right. But just for a little bit."

Gradually, step by halting step, Wander walked up the outcropping. It was so narrow. With every breath, every step, Wander was certain that this would be the last one, the last moment before Wander got to test that oh-so-hilarious theory that it wasn't the fall that killed you; it was the sudden stop at the end.

At last Wander came to the end of the outcropping, and stood there at the western edge of Morocco, the edge of the world. The sun blazed down on the calm ocean. As far as Wander could see, all the world was water.

Then Wander looked back at Rashid. "It's beautiful," said Wander. "Thank you for showing me."

Wander took a step—and slipped.

The world rushed, blurred. Already the water and rocks below looked so much closer—

Then the world was righted again.

Wander stared not at the ocean to the west, not at the rocks and surf below, but at the proprietor, and his calm, steady, but wide eyes.

His left hand held Wander's arm, and he pulled as Wander slowly stepped away from the outcropping, back onto the charred yet solid rock of the promontory.

"Are you okay?"

Wander shrugged. "Whatever I am, it beats being dead."

"I'm sorry."

"No, I'm relieved you were here. It wasn't your fault I slipped." Wander shrugged. "Trouble is—"

"I see it too," said the proprietor. "It looked so similar, but this isn't the place from the painting."

"The sky is too blue."

"The sea is too calm."

"I don't see any land beyond the water. Just more ocean."

Rashid held up his hand. Brown skin glistened in the sun. "Plus, in the painting, the reaching hand is wearing a glove. My hand is bare."

"Still," said Wander, "it is beautiful up here."

"And you faced a fear."

Wander nodded. "I even nearly died. At least there's a story in that. As birthdays go, this is shaping up all right after all."

3

———

SHADOW

The proprietor led Wander back down the promontory. On the beach once more, they shook hands.

"I must return." Rashid sighed. "I can't put off the bathroom any longer."

"Best of luck," said Wander.

"You as well," said the proprietor. "Whenever you leave here, wherever your journeys take you next, if ever you do find out where the place in that painting is, please write and tell me. I must know."

"I will." Wander smiled. "Though hopefully I'll have better balance next time."

"What will you do now?"

Wander pulled out the map. "A wise old gentleman gave me a map," said Wander. "Who am I not to follow it?"

They shook hands, and Wander watched the proprietor walk back toward the hostel. He stopped once, turning a moment to look back at Wander and wave. Wander waved back. Yet as the proprietor looked away, then looked back once more, Wander again felt what seemed like a sadness, a deep regret, as if the proprietor held some secret that he longed to share but could not.

Then he was gone.

Wander turned away from the ocean and read over the map again—but then looked back at the ocean. Go one way, and Wander could ignore the map, head along the beach, have some time by the ocean. Maybe take a dip in the warm waters.

Wander looked down again. Or Wander could follow the map. And see what the old proprietor had in mind.

Usually it would have been so simple. Wander didn't follow paths. Just went—paths be damned.

But today... today... Wander kept looking at the map, unable to pull away. Today there was something about the map. The odd place it led to. Wander looked from the paper to the reality it represented, and grinned.

East of the hostel, far from the sea and the sand and the promontory, lay a small forest. The trees were surprisingly tall and broad. Once past the sentinel trees on the perimeter, the air was cooler, the world a little dimmer, but the sun was high in the sky. While there were shadows, there still was much brightness.

Until Wander passed a tree, and emerged from the forest into a strange grassy clearing, ringed by trees.

Empty except for the center, where two trees stood. Though the other trees in the forest were in full leaf, these trees were bare. Where the other trees were reddish-brown, the bark of the two trees was silvery gray, and the trees were much shorter than the other, perhaps only twice as tall as Wander. Their branches were gnarled and knotted, like hands reaching, and the branches pointed upward, clawing at the sky. The trees tapered into sharp points at the top. Wander wondered how many inattentive birds must have been impaled on those false perches.

From each tree, a little above the top of Wander's head, one branch rose like an outstretched arm, the only branch on each tree to have grown outward instead of upward. Each branch ended in a simple point, so that the two trees seemed to be pointing at each other.

Though the surrounding trees were dimmer here, sunlight filled the clearing and covered the two trees.

Yet a shadow hung beneath the outstretched branches. It almost seemed to ripple, to flutter even. A strange hum filled the air, along with a scent and taste like blood and iron, like lightning and that moment of absolute everything that you can feel only at certain times, like your first kiss or the first time you think you're going to die.

Part of Wander's mind screamed for turning back, for running back to the hostel. It was like the promontory all over again, only no heights and no falling, yet the same fear—

But birthdays were days when anything could happen.

Wander stopped. Breathed. And remembered.

Weeks before this day, Wander had gone to Thailand. There, Paithoon had taken Wander back into lost teenage memories, on a dream quest to fully recall the day the fiery tornado had destroyed Wander's world. But the tornado had also left a message. That message, above all, was what Wander had needed to remember. Once Wander knew the message, Wander had made a promise. Wander would live the truth, no matter what. Wander would choose.

Wander wondered if the choice was here. If the choice was now.

Wander approached the strange shadow, hanging from the branches like a dark doorway.

Wander stepped through the shadow—

And at that moment, everything changed.

4

———

THREE TREES

It was cold. And wet. And not sand.

And shaking.

The earth rumbled. Smacks and cracks rattled in the air, followed by soft *fwumps*.

Wander's eyes opened. The sun was gone. So was the smell of sea air, and that scent the world has when it knows the constant shine of the sun. And Wander was no longer having a nice wee birthday walk. Wander was facedown on the ground. Nose tickling from wet blades of grass. Moss on hands and face.

The earth shook again, then calmed. Wander lay there, counting breaths, counting hopes. Nothing made sense. Panic scrabbled, trying to take control. Wander kept breathing. Kept trying to keep the panic at bay. A broken branch fell to the soft ground.

The earth stayed calm. For the moment. A weight pressed down on Wander's back—the daypack. That was still there. Wander pulled in a breath, must have gotten a little winded from... from whatever had happened. A few bumps and bruises announced their presence, but with modesty. No severe injury.

Raising head. Looking around. Quiet. So quiet. Not a breeze.

No people. No sounds of animals. The world seemed muffled. Maybe it was the clouds, so low Wander could have batted at them like a cat. Maybe it was the mist that clung to the world like a damp shirt. The trees were different too. Buds covered them. It was late winter or early spring here. Wherever here was.

Wander was definitely not in Morocco anymore.

But if not there... Then where was here?

Left arm braced, Wander braced the right arm too—and screamed.

The shoulder pain tore through Wander's body and mind. Wander slammed back onto the ground, face smacking the earth, nose stinging. Wander lay there for a few minutes, feeling the pain, feeling the bright loud wall in the mind that came with any movement from the right arm.

But it was just pain. Left arm braced, hand on the ground. Pushing up from the damp earth. Gasping, but at least sitting on knees and not lying down. The right shoulder screamed again, but with gritted teeth Wander straightened up and looked around.

A grove of trees. Oak. Ash. Birch. The low, misty sky. Like somewhere Wander had gone to before, some other stamp in the US passport, but more trees than were found in Wander's birthplace of Kansas. Something was familiar about this area, but that could be figured out after the pain was stopped.

Wander dug out an extra t-shirt from the daypack and fashioned a makeshift sling. It wouldn't help much, but it was better than nothing. For now. Hopefully the ground wasn't too rough, or some semblance of civilization not too far away. Arm tucked, Wander gritted teeth again and stood. The pain from the shoulder was still there. Tensing the muscles brought fresh explosions, but it was manageable. At least, it would just have to be.

There was no road, but there were still journeys to take from here to there.

Wander just preferred knowing where here was, even if there remained a mystery.

One step in front of another. Wander focused on the walking, tried to ignore the pain. A rough but well-used path led from the clearing in the middle of the trees, through a small wooded grove. Wander stepped carefully, trying to minimize the bumps to keep the shoulder from exploding any more than necessary. The forest air hung damp and heavy with the scent of moss, decaying leaves, and recent rain. Drops glimmered on the branches.

Outside the grove of trees, a bare world greeted Wander. Covered with scrubby plants and speckled with gray rocks, a grassless plain ran in all directions toward low hills that ringed the land and the grove, all pale greens and deep browns.

So familiar. But Wander couldn't place it. Beyond the pain, though, something in the back of Wander's mind was searching, pointing, seeking.

The earth shook again. This time it didn't stop. Wander fell, yelling as fresh agony exploded from the shoulder. More branches shattered in the grove. The hills shook. Wander yelled and yelled and yelled, rolling with the shaking, trying to be still, no firm ground to be on anymore. Nothing made sense, and now this, and now more pain, and now, and now—

And now everything became calm. The earth stopped shaking. The hills were still again.

Wander lay there for a few more minutes, trying to count breaths, trying to shift so the shoulder hurt less. Finally, convinced the quake would not return, Wander got up again. Swaying a little from the confusion and the shaking and the pain, Wander again oriented to the hills. A feeling suggested that west was a good way to go. Right now Wander couldn't think of anything better.

Fear still gnawed, though. Panic still scrabbled. None of this made sense. One minute Morocco, the next here. But where was here? How much time had passed? If spring was starting...

Wander stopped.

It had been summer. Twentieth birthday. In summer.

Months lost. No memory. No understanding. Big backpack gone. Just Wander and daypack, in a different part of the world.

The panic took hold.

Wander turned and ran east instead, forgetting every sense, forgetting every consideration and deliberation and instinct and knowledge gained wandering the world. Wander ran past the grove, no longer caring about the shoulder. The pain came, and kept coming, and it fed the panic like coal into a train's steam engine. Ahead the folds of the hills stretched higher and thicker. You could hide there. And maybe never come out.

A narrow fold caught Wander's attention. Turning toward it, the traveler ran full out. Maybe there was a cave to hide in. Maybe a little stream for water. Maybe anything that could give an indication of where here was and what the hell was going on.

Almost to the hill.

From out of the folds of the hill, a man appeared. Ragged. Covered in scratches. His clothes were faded tatters, and dust covered his brown skin.

Yelling, Wander ran too fast to stop.

They collided and fell to the ground.

5

RAGGED

range. Whatever the ragged, tattered stranger had been wearing, it had been orange. Scratches covered the man. If he were wearing much of anything now, it was blood.

Was it his?

Shoulder throbbing, Wander yelled again.

The man stood up first. For all the confusion on his face, his eyes held a steady, piercing fire. And he was looking at Wander. Something about that gaze wasn't right. Too much fire. Too much seen over too much time. That was the problem. Those eyes held too many years. Yet there was a darkness there too, a darkness that went beyond the deep, rich, brown-black of his eyes. It was as if it had also been a long time since he had seen anything at all.

Then the man smiled. He looked relieved, as if this were the grandest surprise he never had been expecting. He extended his right hand. "The light is so bright when you haven't seen it for so long," he said, and his voice was steady and deep. "I didn't see you. You're hurt. Let me help you up."

There was an accent there too. Irish? But his face didn't look Irish. He looked like he could've come from Lhasa, not Limerick. None of it made sense. Wander tried to breathe deeply, tried to turn down and ignore the pain. The man was a mess. Yet beneath the mud, dust, and rags, he seemed thin yet solid, a winter-ragged bear depleted after a long hibernation. Strength radiated from him. Rippled with muscles, but not like a bodybuilder—like someone who could easily lift one.

"I'm sure I look horrible," said the man. "I'm sorry I scared you."

Wander started to answer, but before Wander could say anything, something about the man began to change.

As Wander watched, all the scratches closed up. The blood faded. Before Wander the tattered man stood healed, his brown skin dirty but unblemished, from the tops of what had been bleeding feet to the crown of his bald head. If there had been sunlight he would have been gleaming, though even as it was he almost seemed to shine.

Except for one thing.

The man's left hand. Wander stared, mouth open, at the scarred, misshapen, twisted mess. The right hand, still outstretched, was perfect, strong. But the left—

Wander almost yelled as the pain hit again, but ignored it and fought to stand back up.

The man glanced at the mangled left hand, as if seeing it for the first time.

"Oh," he said. "That does look rather a mess."

"What the hell are you?" shouted Wander.

He looked up at Wander. "It's okay," he said. "That's supposed to happen." He reached out, but Wander turned and ran.

"Wait!" shouted the man. "Wait!"

Wander kept running.

"Hey!" he shouted again. "What year is it? Are there others?"

6
____

100 YEARS

Away from the hills Wander ran, away from the ragged man. Everything was wrong. What had happened? Kidnapped? Drugged? Wander tried not to think of what else might have happened during however much time had passed unremembered.

Between the pain in the shoulder and the terror in the soul, Wander saw nothing but what was right ahead. Past the grove of trees Wander ran. This time not continuing west, like before. Wander took another path, going north.

Chancing a glance behind. No one followed—but there was a speck in the distance. The ragged man? Wander hoped not, but knew it likely was. Couldn't tell if he was pursuing, though.

Facing forward again. Nothing but gray rocks and stubby brown ground. And the smell. And the familiar look of the place. Maybe it was—

A woman appeared.

From around a bend she had come. She wore a long gray cloak, and her long, unbound hair was both silver and red. In one hand she carried a long, thin, brown walking stick that came up to her shoulder.

"Help me," said Wander, stopping as the woman came near. "Please... help me."

The woman stopped. Surprise showed on her exhausted face, yet she seemed suffused with a light, a peace, and that gave Wander hope. "What is wrong?" Her accent reminded Wander of western Ireland. The woman's tiredness vanished, and her eyes sparked with power and determination.

"I..." Wander paused.

What the hell were you supposed to say? Nothing made sense. The truth would sound crazy.

"I fell," said Wander. "My shoulder. Hurts so much."

The woman set down her stick. "You wear such odd clothes," she said.

"Just some quick-drying cargo pants and a t-shirt. Pretty typical backpacker stuff."

"But your backpack—what is this?"

It was like she'd never seen nylon before.

"It's a backpack. That's all."

Wander shrugged off the daypack and set it on the ground, muffling yells all the while.

Standing next to Wander, the woman raised her hands. She moved slowly, all the while her eyes on Wander, as if watching a wounded wild animal that needed help yet also would bolt at the first suggestion of danger.

Wander nodded. "I'm okay. Just... if you can..."

The woman touched Wander's upper arm and made her way slowly along, finally over the joint and the shoulder, then down Wander's back along the shoulder blade. "You've dislocated your shoulder," said the woman. "It's not bad, and I can fix it."

"Are you a doctor?"

The woman shrugged. "I am many things. Including being the one who can help you right here and right now."

"I'm sorry," said Wander. "Please fix it."

"Tell me," said the woman, laying both hands on Wander's shoulder and back, "how many pints of stout could a goose drink if it were flying backward?"

Wander stared at her. "What the hell are you talking about?"

The woman snapped Wander's shoulder back into joint.

Eyes wide, Wander yelled and yelled and yelled.

"Now don't go doing any somersaults for a few days," said the woman, "but I believe you'll be fine."

"No worries there," said Wander. "I'm much too confused for gymnastics anyway."

"What else is wrong?" said the woman. She guided them to a rock and they sat down. "I'll help if I can. My name is Awen. Helping is what I do."

"Hi, Awen... My name is... is Wander." Wander stared at the older woman. She had helped. And everything about her, everything that Wander could sense, said that this person was safe. "Okay, I'll tell you... but I'll warn you... this is going to sound weird." And Wander told her all that had happened. "The last thing I remember is being in Morocco, and taking a walk through the woods. I walked into this weird shadow between two trees. The next thing I remember is waking up here. In that grove of trees down the path."

Awen nodded. "You're definitely not in Morocco anymore, Wander," she said. "You're in Ireland."

"Ireland?"

"Yes. The region of Connemara, to be exact. West of New Galway. We're a little east of the town of Clifden."

"Galway!" said Wander. "I love Galway. Such a beautiful place."

Awen's eyes narrowed but she said nothing.

"And Clifden," Wander continued. "I took a little side trip up to there. No wonder this looks familiar. The smell... Peat! And the hills. But how the hell am I in Ireland? Oh, wait..."

Opening the daypack, Wander reached inside. "I can't believe

I didn't think of this before. Then again, I was in a lot of pain." Wander pulled out the flip phone and opened it. "Okay, show me exactly."

The screen was dark.

Wander pressed the power button. Nothing.

"Maybe it broke when I fell," said Wander. "Damn. I was hoping the GPS would show me exactly where I am."

"GPS?" said Awen. "You do sound like you could use one."

"A global positioning satellite?" said Wander. "You bet. And my mapping app. Sheesh, I'd almost settle for starting a Facespace account right now."

"I don't know what any of that means," said Awen. "What's an app? Is that short for apple?"

"In a way," said Wander. "But what do you mean you don't know what that means? Social media. GPS."

"Here, GPS stands for Galway Pradesh Stout," said Awen. "It's a beer."

"Okay," said Wander, "then maybe I really could do with one of those. Do you have a phone on you that I can use? Or maybe wifi?"

"Phones have cords and wires and are in buildings," said Awen, "and I'm nobody's wife."

"Not wife. Wifi. Wireless. It's for the internet."

"Enter what net? Are you supposed to be fishing?"

"No... look, it's 2018," said Wander. "How could you not have seen a phone? I mean, yeah, mine is pretty antiquated, but it's still a cell phone."

"Two thousand eighteen?" said Awen. "That's not the year. It's AB 100."

"One hundred? What the hell is A-B?"

Awen sat back, her eyes narrow. A darkness passed over her face. "You really have no idea, do you? AB means 'After Blast.'"

"Blast? What blast?"

"You said that the last thing you remember is going for a walk in Morocco, and then you woke up here in Ireland?"

"Yes."

Awen nodded. "I have to think about this. Will you trust me to help you?"

Wander shrugged a shoulder and winced. Should've shrugged the other one. "I don't know that I have much choice."

"That'll do," said Awen. "Now, why were you running?"

"Okay, this might sound crazy too."

Awen grinned. "I can assure you that I've heard worse."

"I was trying to figure out which way to go, but I came across... I came across... near the hills... I... He..."

Awen sat up suddenly, as if someone had poked her with a pin. "Did you see a man?" she asked. "Covered in rags? Bald head?"

"Yes," said Wander. "He was covered in scratches and dust. He was all bruised, like a building had fallen down on him. I ran into him... then, right before my eyes, all the scratches, all the bruises..."

"Healed," said Awen, nodding.

"I... I panicked," added Wander. "And ran."

Awen nodded. "Understandable. Especially given you don't know him."

"Wait," said Wander, standing. "You mean you do?"

"I do. He's a friend."

"Well, he looks like hell."

"You would too," said Awen, "if you'd been asleep for the past century."

"What are you talking about?"

"He was hurt, quite badly. I hid him away, not knowing whether he would live or die. Frankly, even after all this time, I still didn't. Then with the earthquake earlier, I feared the worst. But at least he's awake. Alive. And made it out of the cave."

Of course. An earthquake. After Wander had... landed. Arrived. Appeared. Whatever the hell it had been.

"Are you saying that this earthquake happened after I arrived?"

"At the same time, from the sound of it," said Awen, standing. "It's a funny ole world. Odds are, you arrived at exactly the moment he woke up. How curious."

"Why was he so hurt?"

"When he's ready," said Awen, "perhaps he'll be willing to tell you himself."

Awen nodded past Wander's shoulder, and Wander turned. Coming up the path toward them, the ragged man walked.

"He's safe," said Awen. "Well, he's also incredibly dangerous, but only to anyone who is a threat to life and the world. Otherwise he's rather a sweetheart. Can talk your ear off, but he's always good company."

"Who is he?" said Wander.

"I'll leave the introductions to him. When he's ready. And when you're ready too. But I'll tell you this for now. Ragged and worn as he may look, that man is ten thousand years old. He's saved the world countless times. And he's the truest friend a person can have. No matter what, he seeks right and truth—and makes it happen, no matter what. He's the hero of old, and it may be, it just may be, that he's back to be the hero of now."

Wander took a few steps back. "This is too much. You want me to believe... that he's as old as civilization... that he's been asleep for a century... which means, if he came to you and you helped him... then you're... not human... you're... what are you?"

"I'm safe, dear," said Awen. "That's all. No, I'm not human in the sense you might think of it. And neither is he. We both have long lives." Awen patted her hair, and ran her fingers down some strands that were more silver than copper. "But as you can also see, my longevity is not as long as his." She looked into Wander's eyes. "It's a lot to take in. You don't know where you are. You just got told that there are things that are real that you never could have imagined could be real. And now, after all that, I'm asking you to trust me. You are too smart not to be scared and wary. But still, I'll ask you—please, Wander, as you trusted me enough to ask for me to help you, please trust me that you are safe."

"And if I don't?"

"Your choice is yours." Awen shrugged. "You can't choose a path until you're standing at the crossroads. But I would hope that you would at least return the favor and, should I ask it and you are able, help me."

Wander looked away a moment. That was the code of the road: Travelers helped each other. Stood by each other. Watched each other's backs. You couldn't be a traveler if you couldn't trust those around you, couldn't find ways to trust those who deserved to be trusted. At least, Wander hoped that worked the same way here. Wherever here was, with its weird years and its people who were really, really old.

"Okay," said Wander. "I'll trust you. As much as I can. As weird as all this is, I don't know how much choice I have right now anyway."

Awen smiled. "You're a traveler," she replied. "Just think of it as another journey, another adventure, and it will work out."

Wander couldn't help but smile a little. But the smile soon faded.

The ragged man reached them.

"You remembered," he said to Awen. Despite the dust and wariness and sadness there, a smile lit up his face.

She smiled. "Always, old friend." She patted his hand. "Always."

The man turned to Wander. "I'm sorry I scared you. I can see where I would have. I don't know you, and you don't know me. But I'll trust you for now, if you'll trust me. You're safe."

Awen looked from one to the other. "Wander has come a long way and has quite a story to tell," she said. "As do you." Awen looked over the man. "Once you've cleaned up, anyway. And had a proper beer in front of you."

The man smiled. "Then lead the way, my friend."

"Sure," said Wander. "Lead on."

Awen turned and came back down the path, and the ragged man and the wanderer followed.

7

GLOVE

The trio walked through the hills and across the peaty ground. The mist had lifted somewhat, and visibility was better. In the peat, Wander could see rectangular marks from where people would cut out bricks of the peat for fires at home. The walk was silent, and Wander was glad for some time to just think, just try to make sense of what was happening. Awen walked between Wander and the ragged man. The older woman's face held both relief—that the man, the ancient hero, was awake and alive, Wander presumed—but also perplexity and worry, as if even greater burdens now weighed down on her.

But what were the burdens? Wander looked around. This place was peaceful. Yet...

How were there no cell phones, or even landline phones? How was there no wifi? And how did GPS mean a beer, instead of a way to triangulate at a moment's notice all the places nearby where you could get a beer?

None of it made sense. Even the year was different here. Wherever here was. It wasn't the Ireland that Wander had been to only a few months prior. It came back to Wander, those times before the hostel in Morocco, before the birthday walk. Those had been mere hours ago, yet a lifetime now stretched between then and now. Wander thought back further, to the Ireland that Wander had been to before Thailand, before crossing west across Asia and Africa. But in Ireland, in Galway, there had been a city that Wander had fallen in love with. There had been music in the pubs at night, and the rich taste of the pints of stout.

And there had been that one traveler, that one person that Wander had, for the first time on the road, after five years, felt connected to. They had met and spent many days together, different paths briefly converging before they came yet again to a crossroads. That person had told Wander about Paithoon, the dream guide in Thailand. Wander rushed to the other side of the world, hoping at last to find and confront the pain from that horrible day in Kansas when Wander was fifteen. The fiery tornado took everything—Wander's mother and father and siblings, the farm they lived on, the nearby town that was home to Wander's friends and school. All burned and gone. Nothing of Wander's childhood world remained. The tornado took everything, but it left a message.

Remembering the truth had taken fear, blood, and utter devastation of Wander's soul, and a reliving of all the death and destruction in Wander's past, but Wander had found the tornado's message again. Now Wander had to live it: Accept the truth. Live it. Follow it. No matter where it led.

Apparently, it had led here.

Some birthday.

Wander wondered what Awen and the ragged man would think of what had happened.

As crazy as the rest of this had been so far, suddenly those times seemed normal.

They came around a bend in the path, passing around a short hill. Once they cleared the hill, the path wound toward a small white cottage, sitting in front of some trees and a clump of low hills. The cottage was one story, with a thatched roof. Left of center was a simple wooden door, with a window to the left of that door, and two windows to the right. From a chimney on the right side, smoke wafted into the morning air.

"Home is where you feel home," said Awen, opening the door and showing them in. "Welcome."

Inside, the simple home was one large room, though at the back was an open doorway that seemed to lead to a separate part of the cottage. On the far wall was a small kitchen, with a low counter separating the kitchen area from the rest of the cottage. To the right of that, in the opposite back corner, was a raised platform that held a simple bed. In front of the entry area were chairs and a spinning wheel. Along the right side wall was a large fireplace where a peat fire brought not only warmth but also a pleasant earthy smoky aroma that was relaxing and welcoming. A massive kettle sat on a wrought-iron platform in the fire.

The cottage reminded Wander of another life, a life that had ended five years ago on one horrible day.

Everything about the cottage said it was a place of peace and calm, a place of welcome and rest. Except for the pillar in the center of the cottage.

Two swords hung from it.

But the swords were in black scabbards, and curved, and had round guards—

What were two Japanese katanas doing in an old woman's cottage in western Ireland?

"Thank you for taking care o' them," said the ragged man.

"I should be thanking you," replied Awen as she hung her gray cloak on the pillar. Beneath the cloak, her ankle-length dress was simple brown wool yet decorated with delicate black knots. Simple yet beautiful. "They've come in handy more than a few times."

He started to walk toward them, but she stopped him and shook her head. "Typical man. Before you can muck about with your pointy toys, you need a wash." Awen stepped back and looked at him again. "Thank goodness you woke up in the morning. This could take you all day." She went to the fireplace and brought the large kettle to the man. Pointing toward the door at the back of the cottage, Awen said, "There's a tub out back. Don't come back until you're presentable."

"And what am I to wear?" said the man. "I didn't exactly arrive here with a change o' clothes."

Awen grinned. "We'll hardly want to shock our guest," she replied. "I took care of it. You'll see."

The man took the kettle and left the cottage.

"Right," said Awen. "He'll be a while. I can understand that this is all very strange, so I'll keep my next question simple: Would you like a beer?"

Wander's mouth watered. "That's the best idea I've heard all day." Then added, "It's... It's my birthday."

"Your birthday?" said Awen.

"At least, it was back in my world," said Wander. "Maybe it's not technically my birthday here. But today, the day I started on, I turned twenty. The big two-zero."

"Ah, I remember twenty," said Awen. "I was well on my way to being a forlorn and improper spinster." She winked. "And I was having a grand damn time of it too. Till everything went wrong." In the kitchen Awen pulled down two mugs, and turned to a small wooden cask on a countertop platform. "Jake from the pub in Clifden just brought me fresh kegs this morning. Poor lad. We had one horrible night, too. Someday I might want to consider sleeping. Yet we've got fresh beer aplenty. Thank goodness I had him bring extras."

"Is that... man... being awake reason for a party?"

Awen shrugged. "Hard to say. It could be the beginning of good things for a world that needs them. Most likely it's a harbinger that a long, winding journey is about to unfold, where there will be lots of death and turmoil, where the world will likely often find itself in great peril, and eventually something will happen where all life, all the world, likely all existence itself, will be on an absolute death's-scythe edge of yes or no—and that man, that crazy man you bumped into and ran from—will be the person who determines the answer."

Wander sighed. "I would have been happy with a cupcake."

Awen set the mugs on the counter so the beer could settle. "Something tells me this wouldn't be the first time things in your life haven't gone the way you had in mind."

"No," said Wander, voice softening. "No…"

"They didn't for me, either." Awen brought over the mugs and pointed to the chairs. "Have a seat. Let's see what we can figure out while he's away. There'll be more than enough to talk about once he's back, and I have to figure out what in the world to do with you."

"Am I messing up some grand ancient plan that is now at a critical juncture? Shouldn't that be how things like this usually work? Some random element shows up and throws off everything?"

Awen chuckled. "The point is well taken, but not necessarily. You could be a random element, as you say." Awen handed Wander a mug. "But you may also be the spark. We'll see."

"What spark?"

"That part of the story will be his to tell. For now, I want you to take a long, long drink of that beer. In fact, I want you to finish that pint. Then I'm going to get you another. And then I'm going to tell you what I think has happened to you and why you're here."

Awen touched her mug to Wander's. "Sláinte," they toasted at the same time, looking each other in the eye.

"Ah," said Awen, after taking a long quaff of stout. "You know the custom."

Wander nodded. The mug was substantially less full. "I was in Ireland for a little while. I loved it. Especially the beer. Is this Guinness?"

"What's Guinness?"

"Stout. Irish stout. It's one of the most iconic beers in the world. Been around since 1759, so since it's 2018 in my world, that's two hundred and fifty-nine years of black beer goodness."

"Well, that stout you're enjoying is certainly one of our most iconic beers in the world, but whatever Guinness is, it's not in this world. The beer you're drinking is called Galway Pradesh Stout. GPS for short. I believe there may have been a lad... Andrew Guinness, Arthur, something like that... who served as the brewmaster for First Call Brewing, the company that makes GPS. Our 1759 was one hundred and seventy-five years ago, but in our world Guinness was not invented, as it was in yours. Perhaps because GPS has been around... well, if not since the dawn of humans, then from an early morning happy hour."

Wander took another drink of the stout. The years were strange here—clearly, Wander had traveled through time as well as place—but pondering what year it was would have to wait. The beer. Goodness, the beer. It was similar to Guinness, yet not. There was a smoothness and a roughness, an overlying bitterness and some astringency, with just a touch of sweetness beneath— though it was as if you had to look for the sweetness to find it. It was beer as a metaphor for life. Yet beneath all that, there was something else...

"Try looking into the mug," said Awen.

Wander did. After drinking through the snow-white foam, the beer beneath was dark, inky black. Completely dark. And then—

"What the hell?"

Inside the darkness, a little white gleam glowed. Like a spark, it flared.

Wander sat back quickly and dropped the mug.

The mug fell toward the wooden plank floor. Wander tried to sweep a hand toward it, to catch it, to save it from breaking—

The mug stopped in midair.

Awen had leaned forward, her own mug held up, her other

hand gently gripping the top of Wander's mug. With a smile, she handed it back to Wander.

Looking into the mug again. The little spark was gone. "What the hell was that?" asked Wander.

"Exactly what you saw," replied Awen. "What you needed to see. Take another drink. You are safe."

Wander did. And as the beer settled through Wander, so did something else.

A vision.

Standing on a rock, a blackened, charred rock, and staring out over the sea. Far in the distance, a thin line of land shimmered.

"Whatever you see, is for you," said Awen. "Speak of it only when or if you must."

Wander drank the rest of the beer, and Awen brought more.

"This is a lot to take in," said Wander. Turning away from Awen, Wander looked out one of the windows, the one near the bed. It faced east toward the hills—the Twelve Bens, Wander remembered them being called in another Ireland, in another world. Assuming the name was the same here, anyway. A dozen rolling hills, green and brown, sentinels on the east. The hills Wander had been fleeing to. The hills the man had been coming down from. Now the mist was gone and the clouds had faded away. Rich, golden morning sunlight poured over the hills and into the cottage.

"I'm afraid you'll have more to take in, and at a gush," replied Awen. "Like I said, I'm now going to tell you what I think happened to you."

"Which is what? I didn't just walk through some damn shadow; I managed to find some random doorway that took me out of my world and dropped me into this one."

"And here I was thinking I was going to have to explain it."

"That doesn't mean you're now excused from explaining," said the ragged man in his deep voice.

Yet as he came back into the cottage, the raggedness was

gone. Freshly scrubbed, the man's brown skin glowed, its amber and reddish notes glinting in the morning light. A ray of sunlight caught his bald head, and for a moment it was as if he had a halo —or as if the light had revealed one. His eyes were a deep brown-black, yet in their darkness there was indeed a light—it reminded Wander of the spark glowing in the black beer. The orange rags were gone. Now the man stood all in black. He wore a long-sleeved black silk shirt, untucked, that went partway down his thigh. His long neck rose from a mandarin collar, and knotwork buttons extended down from the hollow of his throat to his broad chest. Black silk pants both flowed from him and clung to him, and at his feet, black boots rose up his ankle, and ties were wrapped around the bottoms of the pants.

Yet no matter how dark his clothes, his eyes still blazed, a shadow about to catch fire.

"You look magnificent," said Awen. "As well you should. The clothes are a gift from my sister in France. There is no finer tailor anywhere, and she wants you to know that should you need replacements, let her know and they will be provided."

"She has done fine work."

"But?"

"It's a far cry from my old orange," replied the man, not hiding the skepticism in his voice.

"It's better than walking around in your skin," said Awen. "Besides, this is what you asked me to do. You told me that should you return, you wanted a suit of black, for you would go in shadows until the time came for you to regain your light."

"Then thank you, my friend. You have taken care o' me far better than I could have deserved."

From the brilliant glow of his face, Awen looked down to the mangled left hand. It was red and pink, with pale white scars all around. It was functional yet slightly misshapen. "Does it hurt?"

"Yes. Especially when the bare skin touches something."

Awen nodded and stood up. "I wondered about that. All those

years, I would check on you. Your body was healing. The burns would fade, the cuts would heal, the broken bones all set cleanly. Everything about you healed to perfection." She gently lifted the scarred hand. "Except this."

"A souvenir," said the man, bitterness giving his words a ragged edge.

"A reminder," replied Awen gently. She raised the hand and whispered a kiss over it. Then Awen's lips kept moving, unseen words passing over the hand.

When she let it go the man asked, "What were you doing?"

"Such as I can," said Awen. "Asking your being to find its way toward healing. Asking all that is you and is within you to find its way toward the balance of light and dark." With a sharp grin, a hard glint came into her eyes. "And giving your hand a bit more dexterity and resilience so it can be more useful and not hurt as much."

"A practical blessing. Sounds good to me."

"There's one more thing for you," said Awen. She went to the small table next to the bed and came back with a thin box, a little bigger than the man's hands.

He opened it, and took out a pair of black leather gloves, thin yet supple.

"As you know," said Awen, "my sister in Scotland is the most skilled leatherworker in the world. These are a present from her. Should you need more, let her know."

The man put on the gloves. They fit perfectly. "Thank you."

Awen smiled. "Do you want the swords now?"

"Not... Not yet," he said, a quiver in his voice. He turned to Wander. "I want to finally introduce myself properly." He bowed, then offered his right hand. "My name is Faddah Rucksack," he said. "Please just call me Rucksack."

"Wander," said Wander.

"Is that how they do names in the world where you come from?"

"How did you know…"

Rucksack smiled. "I can tell by the scent where anyone comes from. You smell similar to this world, but not o' this world. Well met, my friend. If you'll have me for one."

Wander smiled back and shook Rucksack's hand, then bowed to him. "I will," said Wander. "And no, Wander isn't my given name. It's my chosen one."

Rucksack nodded. "Same with me."

He turned to Awen. She handed him a mug of beer, fresh from the cask. "First pint in… how long has it been, Awen?"

"A century, Rucksack."

"Blimey." He took a long quaff of the stout. "I've missed that," he said. "I hope you have an extra cask."

Awen nodded and Rucksack sat down. "Good," he said. "You've got a lot to fill me in on, and Wander too, being new to this world and all. So, Awen of Ireland, what's been going on for the last hundred years?"

"You mean since you showed up here half-dead in the midst of everyone thinking the world was about to end?"

Wander sat. So did Awen, and she began the tale.

8

DECISION AND DESTINY

"There was bloody chaos," said Awen. "On the sixteenth of October, 1834, the last year in that old calendar era—and if we still had that calendar, it would now be 1934. It was an ordinary afternoon one hundred years and three days ago. Then there was an... explosion. A horrible calamity. Today we call it The Blast. It happened not far from here, in Galway. The fires were unimaginable. They burned in a massive area around Galway. North, east, west, and south of there, though, mile-wide bands of fire shot outward from the epicenter, lines of fire radiating in lines of destruction that decimated everything they touched. Villages and forests burned. Rivers and ponds boiled dry."

Wander held the beer mug tightly, feeling like a child listening to a scary story beside a campfire. Except this wasn't just a scary story. This was history, the scariest story of all.

"The flames caused much death and destruction, but not just in Ireland," continued Awen. "The fire crossed the Irish Sea and burned its way across England too. London was completely destroyed. The fires only stopped when they reached the southeastern end of England, at the Channel."

"What? Around the White Cliffs of Dover?" asked Wander.

Awen shook her head. "They used to be called that here, too. The Blast charred the cliffs so totally, now they are called the Black Cliffs."

"You told me... before I went into the cave, that you would do what you could," said Rucksack, his voice tight and his gloved hand clenched around the mug. "There must have been such panic and suffering."

"It was nearly impossible to deal with, and to this day I don't know how we came through without everything falling apart. Ireland was full of starvation, and there were so many wounded people to tend to. When London fell, especially, the shockwaves were felt around the world. The British Empire all but crumbled overnight. People everywhere were terrified. There were riots. There was not enough medical help. The months after The Blast... the world stood on a knife-edge of complete ruin. While the burning may have happened only in Ireland and England, the terror that The Blast inspired threatened to consume the world, a terror far worse, far more complete and destructive, than any mere fire."

"Yet we're sitting here, in your cottage, drinking beer," said Wander. "So, clearly things didn't go that way."

Awen smiled at Wander, but stared straight at Rucksack. "More and more, people around the world began working together. Helping those who needed help. Turning riots into work parties. Leaders arose. People received aid, food, care. I don't know how it all happened. I did my part here, and my fellow Awens—one in Scotland and one in France—did theirs in their lands. But for all its horror, The Blast did something to forge humanity. It smelted something out of us: our fear and our suspicion, our rage and our never-sated need for bloodshed. Together, people put out fires. Together, people began rebuilding, planning, helping."

Awen turned to Wander. "Tell me, in your world, what is it like for Ireland, Scotland, and India?"

"Scotland is still part of the United Kingdom. India has been an independent nation for over seventy years. Ireland got independence early in the twentieth century, but the northeastern corner of the island, called Northern Ireland, is still part of the UK. Ireland's independence was hard fought."

"Things happened quite differently here," said Awen. "Those who had been part of the British Empire—in government, military, business—when they heard word of The Blast, they almost uniformly left their colonies and came home. Nobody cares about empire when home is in ruins. In the colonies, things changed quickly. England tried at first to maintain control. Yet during the year AB 0—or what you would call 1835—leaders had arisen in Scotland, Ireland, and India. They led those places to independence—in bloodless revolutions. They've been independent ever since. There were similar changes in places throughout Africa, Asia, South America."

Rucksack grinned at Awen. "Three leaders in Scotland, Ireland, and India. Are they still around? Did you happen to know some of them?"

Awen shrugged. "No one knows. They came, they earned trust, they were bold yet kind, and they did what many say were amazing things. Then, independence gained, they left the reins of power for others to take over. Just as they had appeared, they faded away."

"You're telling me that you don't know who that person was? Here? In your own country?"

Awen's eyes twinkled as she considered Rucksack. "Sometimes legend is more important than fact, my friend. Something you taught me."

A corner of Rucksack's mouth twitched upward. "Ever since, you've been running all over Ireland, helping where you can. You took on an impossible job, and you have done admirably. I can't thank you enough."

For a little while they drank their beers in silence. Then

Wander looked from one to the other. "What is an Awen, anyway?" asked Wander. "You introduced yourself as Awen, as if it were your name. But you speak of others like you. Sisters. I don't understand."

"Awen is both name and title," said Awen. "Rucksack found me after The Blast, and it was he who helped make me who I am. He helped me see inside myself, and find a light there, a way to guide and help others. It sounds mystical, and I suppose there are times when there can be a bit of that. I see what needs doing and find a way to do it. Most of the work is far more manual than mystical."

"But there are more o' you now?" said Rucksack.

Awen nodded. "I went where the light said I was needed. Twice it's taken me out of Ireland. Once it took me to France, and crossing the Channel I saw the sadness of the Black Cliffs with my own eyes. Scorched completely black, like a shadowy rip in the world. In France I found another woman who had a light inside, like you found in me. She became an Awen as well, and she is in Brittany. Another time, the light took me to Scotland. There, on the Isle of Lewis in the Outer Hebrides, I met a woman who also had the light. She became an Awen as well, and remains in Lewis. Our lights have us working in our own countries, but we can always come to each other if we are needed."

"If you found those two," said Wander, "could there be more of you someday?"

"Perhaps," said Awen. "It's up to the light and the person who has it. It's no easy job. I'm amazed we have three."

"Yet from what you say," said Rucksack, "the world is rebuilding. People are settling conflicts with words, not weapons."

"Over the past year, I've even been able to be home more, and it has been a restful time." Awen sighed and chuckled. "But I knew it wouldn't last. Something was coming."

Both Wander and Rucksack sat up in their chairs.

"No, not the two of you," said Awen. "I suspected Rucksack

would return but never knew when. Wander, you are a total surprise. No, this is something else."

"What is wrong?" said Rucksack.

"I've been feeling... unsettled. It's as if there is a shadow, growing, stretching, wanting to cover the world. Except I can't find it. I can't find its source. I can't even find the effects of it, necessarily. There's just been a darkness these last months. More conflicts. More tension. Something that seems wrong. The world is holding, but I don't know for how long."

Awen stood. "And that brings us to what is going to happen next."

"And what is that?" said Rucksack. "A quest to find this shadow? A good romp to get me back in heroeing shape?"

"You are putting a good face on it," replied Awen, "but I see the guilt in you, Faddah Rucksack. It is eating at you. You blame yourself for The Blast. You suffered greatly and you lost dearly. Ten thousand years of helping the world, yet you fear that one mistake in one moment has destroyed you. You've been away for a hundred years, and now you know the scope of the suffering the world has endured. I think you have a path, though, and I'm glad you came back."

Rucksack looked away and his voice was faint. "I almost didn't."

Awen nodded. "You saw your father's skeleton."

Rucksack nodded. "In the cave... when I woke... the devastation, the pain, the guilt, all came back to me. Then, seeing him... When the earthquake began, I lay down and considered just letting the cave fall in on me. It was what I deserved. So many died. Because o' me. It was wrong that I should live."

Wander looked at him. "But you didn't. You chose to live."

"Yes, but I don't know what for," he replied. Wander could see it now: the pain, the sense of utter loss. "The Blast happened because I failed to prevent it. It nearly killed me. It should have killed me. The destiny that I have been living for, the purpose that I have lived for... it's gone. It burned in The Blast."

"We can't always choose our circumstances, but we can choose what to do with what happens to us," said Wander.

"Spoken as one who has known loss." Rucksack's voice was quiet and kind as her looked at Wander.

"More than my share."

"Exactly," said Awen. Her voice was kind, but underlying that kindness Wander heard an authority, a resolve.

Then Awen turned to Wander. "Tell me, traveler, what do you want?"

"I have no home but the road," said Wander. "Whatever brought me here, look, I didn't exactly have anything holding me to where I came from. I'm in a new world. I'd like to get to know this place. I may not have chosen to come here, but I can make the most of being here."

"Then that makes our way clear." Awen stood before them. "Though I must ask: If you could go back to your world, would you want to?"

Wander shrugged. "I am where I am, so that's where I am."

"Fair enough," said Awen. "I know of no way to send you back to your world, so all's the better that you'd like to stay awhile. In the meantime, perhaps you can help me. I must find the source of this shadow, this threat of evil, and try to stop it before it puts the world at risk. And Rucksack, you need to see how the world has changed, not just hear about it from an old friend. You have to find a new purpose. You chose to live for a reason. We need to find that reason."

"So we will go on a journey," said Rucksack. "A quest to find what we need to find: a shadow and a path."

"But we have no idea where to start," said Wander.

"*You* have no idea where to start," replied Awen. "This isn't your world." She winked. "But I have some guesses. They may be wrong, but they're a first step."

"When will we leave?" asked Rucksack. "Where will we go?"

"Tomorrow at dawn. Tonight I have some questions to ask, and in the morning I'll have some letters to send," said Awen. "As to our road... I will show you that when the time is right. For now, though..." She walked to the pillar and took down the swords, then walked over to Rucksack. "You entrusted these to me, and I thank you. They have been most useful—especially their little enchantment that conceals them from sight while being worn. But they are yours, and it is time you had them again."

Rucksack stood up.

"Faddah Rucksack," said Awen, "I return Decision and Destiny to you. May you serve them well."

Rucksack reached for the swords, but in the moment before touching them he pulled back and shook his head. "I can't," he said. "I can hardly make sense o' anything yet. This world. What's happening. Last thing I can do is put these to good use."

Awen sighed, but she didn't argue with him. "You have to take them back eventually."

He nodded. "When I'm ready."

"Then you'll need to get ready. I'll wear them for now, Faddah Rucksack, but the time will come—and sooner than you think—when you're going to need to wield Decision and Destiny again, and when you will be the only one who can."

"Tell me," he said, "did you ever figure out which one was which?"

"Nope," said Awen. "I figured if I were using what I thought was one, it was just as likely to be the other."

"Pity," said Rucksack. "I was hoping if you had figured it out. Then you could tell me."

PART II

9

RUIN WEST

The next day the trio rose early and left the cottage at dawn. Swords strapped over her back, Awen led them east, up the Twelve Bens toward the top of Binn Bhán, the tallest of the twelve. The morning was bright, and birds sang as they walked through the green and brown hills.

As they neared the top of Binn Bhán, Wander stumbled.

"Are you okay?" asked Rucksack.

"I was trying to ignore it," said Wander, "but I'm... I'm not keen on heights. Guess I'd hoped that got left behind when I fell into this world."

Rucksack touched a hand to Wander's shoulder. "Just breathe. It'll be all right."

"What makes you say that?"

Rucksack smiled and cocked his head. "It's what works for me."

"You're scared of heights?" Wander looked at him and couldn't help but smile a little.

"Everyone is scared o' something," Rucksack replied. "There was this one time, thought I was going to widdle myself, except I didn't have the time owing to this rather interesting beastie that was rather well endowed in the claws and fangs department. There we were, battling away at the top o' this tall feckin—"

Awen stopped. "We're here."

The three of them stood at the top of the hill. Rucksack took a deep breath and muttered, "Oh feck."

Wander touched Rucksack's shoulder. Rucksack looked back at Wander, who smiled at him. "Just breathe, Rucksack, just breathe."

Together they stared down over a blackened scar. The mile-wide charred band ran east to west. To the west, the horror ended at the ocean. To the east, beyond the horizon, the wound cut into the earth, all the way to their destination: Galway.

"Had the path been a little different," said Awen in a low voice, "The Blast would have cut through here, destroyed Clifden. We were lucky."

"That," said Wander, trying to find the breath and the words as the desolation displaced even the feeling of terror. "That is part of The Blast?"

"That is Ruin West," said Awen. "The Black Road." She began walking down the hill. "And it is our path."

10

____

ON THE ROAD

As they neared Ruin West, the world became quieter. The hills had been full of morning birdsong, and the buzz of insects enjoying the start of another spring day. Yet here, near the Black Road, nothing sang or moved or lived.

"A hundred years," said Wander, "and nothing has come back?"

Awen shook her head. "Not so much as a blade of grass. I've felt this place, year after year, hoping. Throughout the world, you can feel the life everywhere. Even when it seems like you are in the midst of utter desolation, life is still there, breathing softly in the background, out of sight but not out of existence. But here, on the Black Road, there is no life. The Blast decimated everything. It scoured the earth, but far worse than that, it burned up the very essence of life from the soil, the air, the world itself. What you see isn't just ash. It is complete, total, and irrevocable ruin. Nothing will ever grow here again."

Now they were at it. Rucksack stopped near the edge of the char. "Why is this the way we have to go?"

"Secrecy," said Awen. "I believe the shadow knows that it is being sought. It may not yet know who or what is doing the searching, but it knows something. Once we are on the road, we will stay on the road. We will walk there, camp there, leaving only if we must. Not just for the sake of our quest, either. Rucksack, you being back in the world isn't something I want to advertise."

"I've been gone a century, Awen," he replied. "As it was I who always made sure that I wasn't even regarded as a literal actual person, but as a legend. You know that."

"Doesn't matter," said Awen. "The Blast is still part of you, in a way that it isn't for anyone else. The shadow or its servants may notice that. They may wonder about it. Anyone who is connected to this evil has an interest in The Blast. They have an interest in that power. You are not yet back to yourself, my friend. You are weakened, scared, guilt-ridden. If that enemy finds you, I fear what could happen. We are hiding ourselves here. The desolation makes the Black Road all but unbearable, but it also provides a perfect secrecy. Being here will be hard... but it may also save our lives."

Wander stood at the edge, staring up and down the length of it. "Seeing it is horrible enough," said Wander, "but you can't even see across it, it's so wide."

"Once you're on it," said Awen, "don't look for things to improve. You will be walking on hell. I'm sorry to bring you to it, but it is the only way for us to pass safely and inconspicuously while Rucksack regains his strength. Seeing the road is one thing. Walking it is something else entirely."

With that, Awen closed her eyes a moment, took a deep breath, and stepped onto Ruin West.

Both feet on the Black Road, Awen closed her eyes again, and kept breathing deeply. She looked as if something horrible were crawling on her, but she was determined not to break, not to run away screaming. At last, she opened her eyes, and even tried to smile. "I can imagine how I look," she said, "but if I can do it, so can you."

Wander sighed. And breathed. And stepped onto the road.

The world changed.

The sky became the earth. The world turned, and at the same time felt both upside-down and turned on one side. Wander stumbled. The air thickened. The sun vanished. The silence became so total that Wander couldn't find the sound of heartbeat or breath, and even thoughts seemed not to have a voice anymore.

Wander's eyes closed. It was too hard to see, and everything that was there to see was just too horrible. Wander felt a sense of falling. Fading into the black. Becoming not flesh but ash. Giving up seemed imminent. It was too horrible. It was all too horrible. There would be no home. There would be no anything. The world's sounds, sensations, all faded, became muffled, then were gone. No breeze brought the wish for the cool scent of rain. No touch of mist upon the skin. No sounds, of Wander's breathing and heartbeat, of Awen's powerful, calm voice, of Rucksack's striving and hope and passion. All gone now.

All sense and motion left, and a stillness came in. There would be nothing else now. Only that stillness, only that void, only—

Then there was light.

Wander's eyes opened. Awen's hands were on Wander's face. In the midst of all the darkness, all the decimation, there was a spark, a little gleam in the dark.

"No matter how total the darkness," said Awen, "you can find a light." She smiled. "And if you cannot find a light, then you know what you must become."

"I can't find light anymore."

"You can see it."

Wander nodded. "I see only what you bring."

"That's what people always get wrong about me," said Awen. "They always think that I am bringing them light in their darkness. But I'm not. I'm not bringing you light, I'm showing you light. Not mine, though. Yours. I'm not a light, Wander." She smiled. "I'm a mirror."

And with that, Wander understood. The darkness fell away. The little gleam inside Wander got stronger again, could shine again. Even though the world was still thick and desolate and dim, there was still light. There was breath, heartbeat, togetherness. Where there was hope there was life, and where there was life there was hope.

"Just take a step forward," said Awen. "It won't be easy, but it will get easier."

"A journey of a thousand miles," began Wander.

"Begins with a single step," Awen finished. "We have the *Tao Te Ching* here too."

Wander took a step, and then another. With each moment, Wander remembered the light. Remembering made the light brighter. Wander turned and smiled at Rucksack. "You can do it, mate," said Wander. "Let's show this Black Road who's boss."

Rucksack was pale but he nodded. Then he too stepped onto Ruin West. He set down one foot. Then another. He sighed. Started to smile.

Then crumpled and fell.

"Rucksack!"

Wander and Awen ran to him. He lay facedown on the ash, not moving.

Awen lifted him up, touching his face the same way she had touched Wander's. Awen spoke to Rucksack the same way she had spoken to Wander, but Rucksack just swayed, a flopping rag doll in Awen's arms. His eyes were open, but had rolled up into his head, the whites flashing and trembling.

"You can do this," said Wander. "Come on, Rucksack. If I can do this, you can too. Please. Come on!"

"Rucksack!" Awen raised him to his knees, and he sank back like a marionette. Wander could see the light there but felt something else too—heat, and an edge.

"You are ten thousand years old," yelled Awen. "You have saved the world more times than others have crapped. You survived the fires of The Blast. You aren't going to let its damn ash get the better of you, are you?"

Awen grabbed his face and pulled in close to him. "You did not come through fire and death, through the cave, through time, through all that you have known, so you could give in now. You are alive, and you will do, you will fight, you will find a way. That's who you are and what you do." She leaned forward until her nose touched his. "Now damn well do it."

Rucksack's eyes rolled back down, and his pupils dilated as he looked at Awen.

"Fire o' life," he said.

"Yes," said Awen, "that's what the legends call you. Does your fire still burn?"

"Fire o' life," he said again. But he also raised one knee so his foot was on the Black Road. "Fire o' life," he repeated, raising himself from the ash until he was standing again. "No, Awen o' Ireland, I did not come through all I have come through so some ash could do me in."

He looked at them both, and Wander could see tears hanging in the dark eyes.

"But the moment I stood here," he continued, "I could feel it again. All the pain and death. All the burning and screaming. Not just here. But everywhere The Blast touched. I felt it. I lived it. Those who died—people, animals, plants—I was them. I lived and died their final moments. All at once."

Wander took his hand, and Awen took the other. "But," said Wander, "you're still standing."

"They didn't get that chance."

"No," said Awen. "Saving the world is different from keeping the world. You do not control life and death, Faddah Rucksack. Never have, and I hope you never get such ambitions. What you saw was to remind you: What happened, happened—and you still have a lot of work to do."

They said nothing, only stared at each other and at the road. Then they began.

Under the still, sunless sky, they walked for silent hours. The world was not dark, though—only dim, as if lit by a gray glow from the ash itself. They said little, trying to adapt to the barrenness around them, the reminder of so much death and destruction, the ground crunching beneath their feet.

No, not ground.

The death of death. The ash of skulls and homes. The ash and char crunched under their each and every step, incessant, the price of walking on the road. The dull, maddening sound pressed at Wander's skull every time, and every time, all Wander could do was think of that horror that had happened here.

Even the ground had burned in the fires of The Blast, Awen had said. People and trees. Animals and villages. Earth and field and pond and river—and that, Awen had said, was just in Ireland itself.

"Just wait till we get to the shore at the edge of Ireland." Awen's voice was dark. She said no more. Just trudged on.

They were walking on the dead. Nothing was recognizable. No skulls stared out of the ash. There were no bodiless feet in mid-retreat, or the bones of outstretched hands. Actually, Wander realized, some recognizable bones would have been better. That would have been a reminder that there had been life here. This was annihilation to the point of abstraction, as if life had become its own myth.

They walked until what they assumed was nightfall, then took their supplies and made a simple open-air camp. Saying little, they ate and then tried to sleep, hoping that if they dreamed of fire, it would burn only in dreams.

At the start of the second day, the Black Road took them toward the sunrise, or what would have been the sunrise had there been any sun.

When you didn't let yourself think about the need to find and stop some mysterious shadow before it could threaten the world, the plan was simple: On the first day they had walked from Clifden to just outside of Galway. Today they would go into

Galway, said Awen, where The Blast had happened. At the mention, Rucksack had turned pale.

"There is no other way and you know it," said Awen. "Before you can have a future, you must confront your past."

Rucksack did not argue, but it was clear he dreaded the thought. He just moved in a painful silence. Grief and agony hissed in his eyes like water falling onto a fire.

Each slouching step took them closer to Galway. Closer to where so much had ended—and now, thought Wander, where so much more would begin.

11
_____

GIRL

"What do you make of that?" said Awen.

The gloom ahead was winter morning sunlight diluted through used, gray dishwater. Wander stared as far ahead as possible, and finally saw it. An odd shape bumped upward from the surface of the road.

"As long as we're on the Black Road, no one can see us?" said Wander.

"Yes."

"What if someone is on the road with us?"

"Then they can see us and we can see them."

Wander sighed. "I'm guessing that up there is a person who may or may not be out for a morning stroll."

Awen nodded, but her face was grim. She reached over her head to the swords crossed over her back, one hilt rising over each shoulder. Wander couldn't see what she was doing, but she seemed to be fiddling with the guards. "I'm going to go talk to our mystery wanderer," said Awen.

Wander stepped ahead of them. "Let me handle this."

"You?"

"Exactly. Look, I'm new here. Let's use that to our advantage."

They all stopped walking. "Awen, you're this guide and muse, but not everyone wants light—some want darkness. You're concerned about this shadow. Maybe this shadow is concerned about you." Wander turned toward Rucksack. "You're in no state for an outright fight or such right now. Let's just keep you on the down low."

"Down low?" said Rucksack. "Are you saying I should crouch to the ground?"

"Let's keep you secret," said Wander. "I'm just someone. Nobody, really."

"Walking on a road where nobody walks," added Awen.

Wander shrugged. "Yup. And I'm going to meet up with somebody else who is walking on the road nobody walks. I wonder what else we'll have in common."

"But if they intend us harm," said Awen.

Wander shrugged. "Then I'm going to trust that you'll run like hell to my aid."

"Okay," said Awen with a sigh. "We'll try it your way."

Wander went ahead.

With each step, the shadow became more distinct. Even the dim light seemed to brighten a little. Wander assumed that, off the Black Road, the sun was rising into an uncharacteristically, surprisingly beautiful Irish morning.

Then the shadow became not just more distinct—it came closer.

Without thinking, Wander wanted to turn around, to head back, to disappear into the gloom. But Wander thought of Rucksack and Awen: the old hero trying to find his place in a changed world, the guardian of light trying to catch a shadow. Wander's eyes narrowed, and Wander walked faster. If trouble was to be met, it might as well be met head-on.

The shadow faded—and became a face, pale, and set with blazing blue eyes surrounded by long black hair. The young woman seemed about sixteen years old, but even then, her face and frame were thin. Far too thin, thought Wander, for someone acquainted with a balanced diet—or even regular meals. She stood slightly sideways, so that Wander could see only the girl's right arm. Her left side was in shadow.

"I had hoped," said the girl. "Today's my birthday. It's the first time in ten years that I've been allowed outside."

"Outside what?" said Wander.

"Outside of my village."

"I would tell you happy birthday," said Wander, "except you seem to have little to be happy about."

"Perhaps I will," said the girl. "I had to be here. Today. My birthday. I had to hope... It was my last hope."

Rucksack and Awen came up behind Wander and stopped. They stared at the girl.

"What is your village?" said Awen. "For I have never seen such a place as you might have come from. And when was the last time you left?"

"My village is nameless," replied the girl, "for it is a place of dream, as all the world is a dream. Only the real have names. As for when I last left..." She sighed, and for a moment she looked away, her blue eyes seemingly dulled with agonies old and new. She shifted her posture, as if uncomfortable, and kept her left arm out of sight.

"The last time I left," she said, "was ten years ago. I had just turned six. It's when he did this to me."

She raised her arm.

Rucksack took a step back, and Awen's hand covered her mouth. Wander's world turned in circles again.

The girl's left arm ended at the wrist.

Tears burned at Wander's eyes. "I'm so sorry."

The girl shrugged. "I've had a long time to get used to it."

Fear radiated from the girl. But so did something else. Strength. Anger. Power. Fires burning under a placid surface, like magma beneath the earth. But what would happen when it erupted?

"What is your name?" asked Wander.

"We are all nameless," said the girl, "for we are all dream, and names are only for the real. That is what he tells us." The girl's mouth curled upward into a smile, and she leaned forward. "But I do not believe him. I have a name. Even though I do not say it, I whisper it to myself when I go to sleep at night. To remind myself that he is wrong and I am real."

"What is your name?" asked Wander.

"Róisín," said the girl.

"Row-sheen," repeated Wander carefully. "It means rose, right?"

Róisín nodded, and the others introduced themselves.

"Who is this man of whom you speak?" Awen stepped forward, her voice veneered in softness, rage catching fire beneath. "Who thought he had the right to do this, and what did he give as his excuse?"

The girl shrugged. "He was not of our village. Ten years ago, he came. None know from where. None know why. He had a smile that could trick anyone. His words were an embrace but they were a snake's coils. We were beguiled by his words, and before you knew it, his will was wrapped so tightly around us all that we could never be free again. He took over the village, and he rules us. We are nearly dead, all but starving. We toil, and we toil, and if we break any of his rules, we are punished."

"What rules did you break?" asked Awen.

"My family was hungry, and we were not allowed food," said Róisín. "So I stole bread. My hand was cut off. Three days later, I left the village to find help. I was brought back, and I was whipped, and I was told I could not leave the village for ten years. If I did, my parents would be killed."

Awen's face was pale, but not with horror. The older woman's eyes were all but aflame, and while her face seemed relaxed, Wander could sense the tensed muscles there.

"What work does he have you do?" said Rucksack.

"He says that we will be the army of the real," said Róisín. "He says that we are a dream in a world of dream. All our suffering, all our pain, all our hopes—all is imagination. He says we are slaves and figments... but he says that there is a place, far away, that is real, and from there comes our dream. He says that one day we will go to this place, and we will be free. The dreamed will become the real."

"Why did you come here?" asked Awen. "Of all places, what brought you here?"

"I dreamed it," said Róisín. "On the day of my birth, I stood on the Black Road and three gifts came to me. Will you help me?"

"Yes," said Awen. "I protect this land, and I strive to bring light where there is darkness. Your darkness has been so total that it hid itself from me. I am sorry, and I will do all I can to help."

"Yes," said Rucksack. "I have been called the fire o' life. My flame is low, but your need is great. I will do all I can."

Wander said nothing.

"Wander?" said Awen. "What do you say?"

Wander stared from the girl to the others. "I don't know this world," said Wander. "I am new here. Where I am from... there is much suffering. Much unhappiness. It's something I've always known was there." Wander looked at Róisín's wrist, then looked the young woman in the eye. "I don't know this place well. But I know that what has happened to you, what is happening to your village, is wrong. I am no warrior, no guard, no guide. I'm just a traveler. But my wanderings have brought me here. If this is where I am and if this is where you need help, then helping you is what I'll do."

"My village is off the Black Road," said Róisín, "but not far."

"Awen," said Wander, "you told us—"

"That is of no importance right now," said Awen. "What will

be will be. We are going where we are needed. Lead the way, Róisín, and we will follow."

They left the Black Road, and Róisín led them through pathless fields and hills. Only rough ground led to the nameless village. After a couple of hours of walking, they rounded a hill and Róisín stopped them. "The village is ahead, but we must not be seen."

Wander peeked out. A tall white wall circled the village. From platforms on the other side of the wall, armed men stood and glared out over the land. Above a wide, tall, wooden gate in the center of the wall, eight men stood in a line.

"We must wait," said Róisín. "Once night falls, we can circle to the far side of the wall, where there is another, smaller entrance. There we can enter, and move swiftly."

"Then we should spend our time talking tactics," said Awen. "Tell us all you can about the village, about what you have in mind, and what things are like."

"We need to know everything," said Rucksack. "This man, for starters. The person who came ten years ago and took over the village. What is his name?"

Róisín shivered. "He has no name that anyone knows—or if anyone did know it, they are long dead by his hand. Now... Now he has only the name he gave himself. He calls himself Scáth."

She pronounced it like "broth" but said it with a chill.

"What does that mean?" asked Wander.

"It's an old Irish word," said Rucksack. He turned to Awen, who nodded, her face as grim as his. "It means shadow."

12

EIGHT PLUS TWO

Róisín told them all she could about the nameless village, about the man Scáth, and about the horrible decade that had passed. Together, the four of them strategized until they had a solid plan.

Róisín would sneak them into the village through the back gate, with a diversion that would preserve their stealth. From there, she would lead them through the rows of small thatched and wooden huts, to the western edge of the village. Against the wall, Scáth ruled from a stone stronghold. No one but Scáth and a few select guards ever went inside. From there, they would have to improvise a way to neutralize Scáth and free the village.

Night fell. They crept by, avoiding the main gate. Róisín watched it as they moved, slowly and silently. Eight guards, all clothed in uniforms of black and silver. And two more people stood in the line. Instead of uniforms, though, these two wore limp, dull, torn gray rags that hung off their thin bodies, which had long forgotten what a full meal felt like. Róisín stumbled. The end of her wrist smacked the ground, and a muffled yelp of pain whooshed through her lips.

"I'm sorry," whispered Róisín, but they kept moving.

Around the back of the village they came, approaching the wall. Wander knew that physically they could turn back. Turn and run. But to do so would be spiritually impossible. Rucksack and Awen would not leave these people to suffer. Seeing Róisín and now these gaunt, starved people, Wander knew that for the soul, there was no turning back—no way to go but forward.

"We're ready for the diversion," said Awen.

Róisín nodded, but even in the dim night, Wander could see a sadness in the young woman's eyes.

"Róisín?" asked Wander. On top of the wall, the guards all watched the people approaching. "Um, we've been seen."

Instead of replying, Róisín ran toward the back gate. "Strangers!" she yelled. "Invaders! They took me, and they have come in the darkness. We must find out what they know! Catch them, catch them now—and beware the old woman. She is armed with two swords!"

The two guards at the gate ran out. Moments later, others followed—and surrounded Wander, Rucksack, and Awen.

Wander stared at Róisín, who stood just behind the circle of guards.

The young woman hung her head and walked through the gate.

13

THE GUARD'S STORY

Inside the rough hut, the ground was damp and the thatch reeked of mold. A huff and a puff could knock down the walls, but the guards outside had been given the swords Decision and Destiny—and the guards looked far too keen to see how they worked. The trio sat on the floor, in the dark, no light but a bit of moonlight coming through a ragged window cut in the back wall.

"We trusted her," said Rucksack, his voice seething. He punched the dirt. "You never know what will happen on a journey, but you have some bit o' confidence that whatever happens takes you toward your ultimate goal. But this..."

"This place is horrible," said Awen. "Those people were so thin. And their eyes... They have known so much suffering." She stared at the doorway. "This place is practically on my doorstep. Near Galway. I've been here before. Not long after The Blast. It was a different place. They took pride in their sheep, and trade was decent. There was music here."

"Do you remember the village's name?" asked Wander.

A silent moment passed. Awen shook her head. "I should be able to. I can remember anyone I've met, from their face to their family. But the name of this place... it's gone. The shadow has hidden not only the village itself, but its very identity."

"Róisín couldn't remember it either," said Wander, voice soft, staring at the others. Wander punched the ground. "She said she wanted help."

"Maybe she wanted bait," said Rucksack. "Or sacrifices. Or torture subjects. She wasn't exactly specific. She betrayed us, Wander. And when we get out o' here, we'll have to remember that." Wander looked at him, wincing at the bitterness pouring from the fallen hero.

"You made a mistake," said Wander softly.

Rucksack stood, and the heat of his gaze singed. "That has nothing to do with this."

"It has everything to do with this," Wander replied, not backing down. "You say The Blast happened because you couldn't prevent it. Because you tried but failed. Preventing things like The Blast—hey, that's what you do. Or did. Or whatever. But this time you didn't, and horrible things happened. You don't trust yourself—and that makes you suspicious of others. Makes sense. If you can't find the best in yourself, how can you possibly see it in someone else?"

"You have no idea what I've been through." Rucksack leaned forward until he and Wander were nearly nose to nose.

"I can't imagine surviving what you've survived, or living with the guilt and memory and pain. Not on that scale. And I won't pretend to know what that's like." Wander's eyes narrowed. "But you aren't the first person to fail or suffer."

"What do you know? Fancy clothes, tales o' a world where everyone has their noses glued to screens and missing the world that's living and doing and changing right by their faces?"

"Ever live through a tornado?" asked Wander.

Rucksack took a step back. "What?"

"A tornado. A funnel cloud. A twister. I assume they happen in this world?"

"They do," said Rucksack. "I've seen them, but never had to deal with one."

"I grew up in Kansas, in the heart of the US," said Wander. "The summer when I was fifteen, I was out walking the land around my family's farm. There was a town nearby. I had walked up to a little hill to look out over the farm, my family's home, and the town beyond. My parents were in the house, along with my brothers and sisters. That home, that town, those people were my world." Wander stepped forward, and Rucksack took another step back, toward the wall.

"As I stood there watching from the little hill, to the east, beyond the town, the sky darkened. A couple of minutes later, a sound like a freight train ripped through my ears. A tornado touched down. Not some little bathtub whirlpool either. It grew until it was over two miles wide. Then it devoured everything it touched. It destroyed the town. No one survived."

"That must have been horrible," said Rucksack.

"It was," said Wander, "but it got worse. The tornado caught fire. It might not have been your Blast, but imagine a two-mile-wide wall of flame, as high as the sky—coming toward you."

Rucksack looked away.

"That hellwall came for my family next. It ate the house, burned it completely. It was so hot that even though my family had gotten underground, they all died. Everyone I knew died. Except for me." Wander leaned in close. "So you look at me, Faddah Rucksack. I survived too. Not just the loss. The tornado. It picked me up, it knocked me around, and it set me down miles away. I survived—practically unharmed. I don't know how. I don't why. But I did. Like you did. I was left completely alone, just a kid in what used to be a cornfield."

"I'm sorry," said Rucksack.

"I know what it is to lose, and to be not just alone but lonely," said Wander. "I don't have long life and instant healing and all this other rot you do. I'm just a person. I've spent the last five years wandering the world—no home, no family, no friends, no roots, no destination. One thing has gotten me through: I keep finding a way to trust people. You can't travel if you don't trust. You say the world is your home? Then trust it. You've been scared but not of the world. You're scared of yourself. You're scared you'll fail again. Know what? You will. Learn from it. Learn this world. Make right what you can make right. If you're this 'hero o' old' and you're trying to figure out what the hell you are now, then you'd best start trusting again. Trust me and Awen. Trust the world. And trust we will not only get through this, but we will keep finding our way. You'll find a new path, but only if you don't give up. Only if you believe again. Starting now."

Rucksack said nothing, only stared at Wander, his expression a mix of fear and pain, but something else was there too—something Wander couldn't make out.

"Okay then," he said at last. "What do you suggest we do?"

Wander took a step back. "I have no idea. Yet."

"I think I can help with that," said Awen. She looked at Wander and gave a quick wink and a grin.

Rucksack and Wander sat back down. The trio began to talk, voices low so the guards outside couldn't hear, and as they talked they began to devise a plan.

They were deep into their discussion, around midnight, when they heard something outside that made them pause. New guards came and relieved the other guards. They also marveled at the swords, and the trio could hear them swinging the blades around, the air whistling as the sharp steel sliced through it. After a few minutes, one said to the other, "I bet the hound is coming."

"He's not gonna send the dog," said the other guard. "It's just a story that only dumbarsed eejits like you believe."

"No, you arse midget," said the first guard. "It's true. I'm telling you, I heard Scáth himself talking about it. The shadow's hound. It's like a magic dog. Only instead of hunting rabbits or foxes, it hunts souls. It can sniff out when something is different about someone. It can find that person for its master. I wouldn't want it hunting me, that's for sure."

"Sometimes I wish we had booze here," said the other guard. "Then at least I could think you were drunk."

"It stops at nothing," said the first guard. "And it does whatever the shadow commands. It's the only thing that scares me as much as he does."

"Only thing scares me is how daft you are."

Awen had looked toward the door while the guards argued. Eventually they fell silent, each finally agreeing that the other was an eejit who didn't know which end of a sword was pointy. Rucksack looked at Awen and nodded. "What do you make o' it?"

Awen shrugged. "I wonder. Stranger things happen. Have been happening for a long time. But since The Blast... there have been many different things about the world. It's as if old magics, old powers and forces, have come back in new ways. And it's as if there are new ones at play too. Every story has an element of truth, and the real often cloaks itself in the fantastic."

They went back to planning. Finally, with grim nods all around, they stood.

"Do you think it will work?" said Wander.

"If it doesn't, at least we'll die quicker," replied Rucksack.

"On three," said Awen. "One... two..."

Outside the ragged hut, muffled thumps and a near-shout, quickly choked off, broke the midnight silence.

Rattly sounds came from the locked door, and then the door opened.

Holding the twin swords, Róisín stepped inside.

14

THREAT

"What the hell are you doing here?" Rucksack's voice was a low growl, like a tiger set to pounce. He had stepped in front of Awen and Wander, turning his body sideways, slowly shifting his stance so that he was ready to attack or defend.

"You have no reason to trust me," replied Róisín. "But I hope this will make a start. Though in case you didn't notice, they're still in their scabbards."

She offered the swords to Rucksack. He stared at them, raised his gloved hands—but shook his head and backed away. "I... I can't."

Awen sighed and took the swords. She didn't cross them over her back. She stepped in front of Rucksack and held them up.

"It's time."

"You don't know—"

"I know that Decision and Destiny need to be where they belong, but that is no longer with me."

"No, Awen."

"I'm sorry for what happened," said Róisín. She handed Rucksack Awen's staff. "Take this instead then, and sort out the swords later. Assuming we have a later. I'll be quick, and then we must go.

When we came to the gate, there were more guards than usual." Her voice trembled. "Then two more people were brought up to the platform."

"The two in the rags?" asked Awen. "The ones who didn't look like guards?"

"They weren't guards," said Róisín. "They were my parents."

Wander stepped forward.

"No." Rucksack reached out, but Wander shrugged him off.

"Why did Scáth put your parents there?" said Wander.

"As a warning. To tell me not to try anything or they would be tormented and killed," said Róisín. "Scáth has always been suspicious of me." She raised her left arm. "Ever since this. Sometimes I think he fears me."

"Tyrants fear what they can't control," said Awen. "He knows that he may have hurt you, but he fears he has not broken you. And clearly he hasn't."

Wander nodded toward the front of the hut. "You have one hand and you just took out two armed men so you can rescue the strangers you only seemed to betray. I can see why Scáth thinks you could be trouble."

"I've never opposed him, not since he cut off my hand."

Awen stepped forward and put her hands on the young woman's shoulders. "He knows you could oppose him," said Awen. "And you are. Every time over these long years that you whispered your name, you were resisting. The moment you trusted your dream and came to the Black Road, you were resisting. You've known all along where this was leading: opposition. Resistance. Rebellion. I can read the path in you, Róisín. You're going to remove him from power or you're going to die trying."

"I don't suppose you can read a bit more than just that?" Fear trembled in Róisín's eyes.

"If only I could, then so many things would be easier," said Awen. "You are scared. You should be. The stakes are high, yet that is also your advantage. Scáth is terrified of you because he fears you. He is not afraid that you will rise up but that he will fall." Awen smiled. "So we'd better move quickly. You won't have another chance like this."

Róisín nodded, then told them the plan. Together, they left the hut.

15

———

SCREAM

From hut to hut the four of them roamed, zeroing in on Scáth's compound. He had to be stopped and they understood this now more than ever. Crossing through shadows, passing by guards, they turned away at the perfect moment, and slipped along the backs of the huts. Other than guards and soldiers, everyone was inside their huts asleep—or wishing they were.

Moonlight brought out the sad village's wretchedness. Every hut looked like a harsh word could knock it down. Then again, thought Wander, harsh words were in ample supply. The people were beaten down, but they kept going. They were broken—but perhaps they weren't beyond repair.

Róisín guided them to the back of Scáth's compound. Awen became the shadows, and the last thing Wander saw of her was Awen raising her hands to the swords on her back.

Wander looked away.

Two soft *thwumps* followed—and so did two more.

Awen returned, both swords again peeking over her shoulders.

"You didn't have to kill them," said Wander.

Awen raised an eyebrow. "What makes you think I did?"

Wander stepped forward. The guards lay on the ground, still but breathing.

"Each sword fastens to its scabbard," said Awen. "Then they can be used like two staffs. It's my preferred method." Awen nodded at Rucksack. "Something I learned from someone who knows well."

Despite himself, Rucksack grinned and chuckled.

They made their way into the compound, avoiding guards when they could—or giving a few guards a good scabbarding to the back of the head when this couldn't be avoided.

Then, outside the double doors to a large room at the center of the compound, they stopped.

Voices came from inside.

"That's Scáth," said Róisín. "But I don't recognize the other. It's not someone from the village."

"Are you truly going to send the hound?" said Scáth.

"Wait," whispered Wander. "Is that the magic soul-hound that the guard was talking about?"

"Your news of these strangers is most interesting," said the voice, which was deep and booming, with a slight rasp. "These last couple of days my hound has noticed something strange, as if something bright has emerged from darkness. Until earlier, we had not been able to divine a location. You have done well, my servant."

Awen's eyes widened. "I should have known," she whispered. "Scáth may be a result of the evil I seek, but he is not the source."

"The hound will be there as soon as possible," said the voice. "This discovery... someone like this in the world... it could be essential to the plan."

"Your servant awaits your servant," said Scáth.

Then silence.

"I hear footsteps, but only one set," said Rucksack. "Whoever Scáth was speaking with, either they are standing still... Or they weren't there."

"Then how could they communicate?" said Wander.

The footsteps they did hear, though, were leading away. Quietly Rucksack opened the door and they all crept inside. The long, narrow room was dim, all shadows and darkness, broken only by a few candles lit here and there near the walls. Scáth walked toward the other side of the room. He was broad, bald, and pale, wearing thick black clothes covered with a cloak, the hood down. From a distance he looked merely fat, but the way he carried himself suggested more muscle than he let on. He stopped before another, identical set of double doors.

"We'll go on three," whispered Awen. "I'll take point. Rucksack, you follow behind me so he thinks there is only one person approaching. Wander and Róisín, stay here unless it's clear you're needed."

"One," said Awen. "Two—"

Scáth opened the other set of double doors. Then he turned and walked a few steps toward the center of the room. Fifteen armed men came inside, and surrounded their leader behind him and to the sides.

"That was well done," said Scáth. "But for all your bravery and stealth, you come not to victory but to a most crucial choice. You could assault me." The men around him drew swords. "Or you might decide, Róisín, that perhaps you should be at home right now, checking on your mum and dad."

Next to Wander, Róisín's face paled.

Then, through the still and silent night, a scream tore all things.

Róisín stood and ran. Awen, Rucksack, and Wander followed.

Behind them came the dry, brittle chuckle. "Take your time, my soldiers of the dream," said Scáth. "Savor this moment. We know where to find them." Scáth grinned, more shadows than teeth. No smile, no light came from his sunken dark eyes. "The hunt can be slow when its end is known."

16

KISS

The village was still silent, but the hut Róisín ran to held a different silence, one that followed not sound but the call of wrong. The call of horror.

The four of them neared the hut. Around them were other stirrings, people awoken by the scream, wondering what had happened, asking themselves if they dared peek outside, when it might risk them making their own same scream.

At the door Róisín stopped first, and the others right behind her. In the moment before Róisín knocked the door open, Wander heard it. The sound that was wrong, in the midst of all that silence.

Another ragged breath came, then faded, and it was wet and torn breathing, the sort of breathing that leaves you grabbing on to thin tendrils for any semblance or sense of life.

"Stay here," said Wander to Rucksack and Awen. Then Wander followed Róisín inside the hut.

The young woman kneeled between her parents. No breath, ragged or not, came from Róisín's father.

From his bare torso, the blood had stopped pouring from the slashes and holes.

Róisín held her mother's hand, and squeezed as the next ragged breath just barely followed the one that had come before.

For the first time, Wander could see not the young woman, but the little girl she had once been. The girl who had wanted to understand the stars, or skip down a village lane in the spring. The girl who had wanted to know she had a place in the world, as she was, and as she would one day be.

"I'm sorry," said Róisín.

"No," said her mother. "We are sorry. You always thought he took your hand because of you. He took your hand because we fought him. You were our example. His threat and his promise."

"I didn't, I should have—"

"You are doing what we cannot." Róisín's mother raised a bloody hand and touched her daughter's face. "Your father has gone. I am going. But our love, my dear rose of the land, our love stays with you. Whether blood or kindness, justice or love, do what must be done. And always know the difference between what you wish would be done, and what must be done."

Róisín's mother sat up a little, just enough to whisper something, briefly, in her daughter's ear. Whatever it was, Wander could not hear, but Róisín's eyes widened. With a weak smile, Róisín's mother kissed her daughter on the forehead. Then she lay back down. Eyes the same star-blue as her daughter's, Róisín's mother stared into her daughter's eyes. Another ragged breath.

Then no more.

Róisín squeezed her mother's hand one more time. She kissed her mother's forehead. She kissed her father's forehead. She traced her fingers over their paling cheeks, over their reddened bodies. Then, Róisín traced a finger over her forehead, then each cheek.

"Róisín," said Wander. "They're coming."

Róisín nodded. In those eyes, Wander saw both the fire of the stars in the deep-night sky, and the ice of absolute decision that lay beyond the floods of grief, the fires of vengeance, and the winds of justice. Just as life had left her parents, the youth left the woman.

Róisín stood and passed by Wander, who followed Róisín out of the hut.

The fifteen guards were nearly to them. Scáth walked a couple of steps behind his living shield. Wander was certain he was smiling.

Róisín stood there, a little in front of and between Rucksack and Awen. Just the four of them—against fifteen guards. And Scáth. Wander had no idea what the villagers would do. Whose side would they take? Or would they take no side, hiding in hope of mere survival?

Wander stood by Róisín. And wondered what to do.

17

SURROUNDED

"I always knew you would be trouble." With a heavy tread and a mirthless, joyless face, Scáth stepped in front of his guards and stood a few feet from Róisín and Wander. He scowled. "Even as a little girl. Thinking you had a right to eat when I said you were to go hungry. Your parents were no better. They believed they could unseat me." He grinned. "Well, that's settled."

Róisín said nothing. The fire still glowed in her eyes, but it flickered, wavering, as if it might go out.

"You have no right to be here," said Wander. "You have no right to hurt and deprive anyone."

"To have the rule is to have the right," said Scáth. "Observe."

Scáth raised his right arm over his head, then extended it forward, pointing at Róisín, Wander, Awen, and Rucksack. "Swords," he said. "Feel free to hack them to pieces. We'll feast on them later."

A hunger blazed up in the starving guards. Wander was certain some of them began to drool.

Awen and Róisín stepped in front of Rucksack and Wander. Awen pulled a sword from its scabbard. The curved bare metal gleamed like a grin. "Rucksack," said Awen, "whether with swords or with staff, please tell me you remember what to do when surrounded by armed soldiers."

"I guess we'll find out," replied Rucksack. His hands trembled, but Wander could see something in the set of his face that hadn't been there before. "Then again," added Rucksack, "I didn't come all this way to leave a git like this in power." He grinned and raised the staff.

Awen looked at Róisín, then drew and handed her the second sword. "I'm pretty sure this one is Destiny," she said.

"I've never used one before," replied Róisín. "Doesn't it need to be held two-handed?"

"You'll manage with one hand, same as I do when I'm using both swords," said Awen. "The main thing is to focus on not dying. That does wonders for helping you figure out where to put the sharp and pointy bits."

"And this works for you?"

"So far so good."

"No more spare swords, huh?" said Wander.

"Get behind me," said Rucksack. "Take up whatever you can think o'. Anything can be a weapon if you think about how you can use it."

Wander stepped back toward the hut. A hut made of thatch—not renown for its ability to fend off a sword.

But if what Rucksack said was true...

Wander pulled a handful of thatch from the roof. At Wander's feet was a rock, small enough to grasp, big enough to leave a mark. Wander picked that up too.

Fifteen against four, the guards pressed forward, slowly, swords out.

"Remember," said Awen to Róisín. "Killing is a choice. Do only what you must. Scáth has twisted them, tormented them, terrified them. But they are still the villagers you grew up with. Try to stop them, but avoid harming them if you can."

"What if I have to kill them?"

"Then do what I do," she said, with a sideways glance at Rucksack. "Don't hesitate."

"Above all," Rucksack added with a grin, "always keep the bastards guessing."

With a yell, Awen ran forward. As she neared the line of men, though, she broke right, toward the end of the line. The sword flashed in the moonlight, and men turned to face Awen, four swords raised against her one.

Rucksack stood near Róisín, trembling, his hot bravado cooling in the night air. Wander wasn't sure if he was going to fight or run. A guard quickened his slow approach to a rush, raising a yell along with his sword and swinging the blade toward Róisín. She stood there, eyes wide, death blazing toward her in glinting moonlight—

The staff knocked away the sword. Another swing of it sent the guard sprawling and unconscious. Rucksack repositioned the staff as more guards neared—then he lunged forward, staff whirling. A man fell. Then another. But another guard got close enough, and soon Rucksack was a blur, fending off sword blows.

"I remember!" he yelled. A boyishness came into his eyes and voice. "I remember!"

A guard neared Róisín. But she still stood there, sword raised in one hand, left arm down at her side. Wander couldn't see Róisín's face, but could feel the confusion there, the paralyzing fear.

The guard was smiling as he raised his sword, ready to cleave Róisín's head in two like a melon.

Then he was stepping backward, coughing, flapping his hands at his face. He dropped his sword and raised a hand to his right eye. Some of the thatch must have poked him, thought Wander, stepping forward, body moving in a manner long remembered from summer days in Kansas. The rock launched like a baseball from Wander's hand. There was a brief, satisfying crunch when it hit him between the eyes, and an even more satisfying thump when he hit the ground and stayed there.

But there was no moment to celebrate. More guards were nearly to Róisín, and Wander was now out of weapons.

Wander grabbed Róisín's shoulders. "Your parents didn't die so you could stand here and do nothing!" Wander yelled. "Your mother told you. You have the strength. You have the courage. For feck's sake, you even have a sword. Now use them!"

Wander stepped back, but one of the guards had gotten too close. His sword swept toward Wander's torso. No time to jump back, no way to duck, nothing to do but die—

A long gash opened up on the guard's arm from shoulder to hand. He yelled and dropped the sword. Róisín swept the sword past him, then used her momentum to swing forward, raise her left arm, and bash her elbow across his face. He staggered backward, but two more guards were there now.

"Get them!" yelled Wander. Wander ducked and leaped forward, under a sweeping sword meant to liberate Wander's head. The fallen guard's sword was near, and Wander lunged.

Steel clashed on steel, and Róisín stepped back and swung the sword again. The guard was grinning. Then he staggered forward, and Rucksack stepped near. Rucksack swung the staff again, but it missed. The guard kicked out, knocking Rucksack away. The guard and Róisín swung and blocked blow after blow, but she was losing ground with every swing.

"You're outmatched, little girl," he said. "Another hand might've given you a better chance." They stepped toward each other, and he raised his sword—

But Róisín got to him first. The sword's end cap broke the guard's cheekbone. Then his face reddened. "I might only have one hand," said Róisín, lowering her left knee, "but two of those didn't do you any favors."

He tried to lift up, but Awen cracked him on the back of the head and he went down. Awen gave a brief nod, and a hint of a smile, to Róisín, then they turned to the other guards.

Wander rose up, sword in one hand. A desperate lunge grazed the hip of a guard. "Crap," said Wander. "I never was good at this. I couldn't even play swords well as a kid."

The guard winced but kept moving toward Wander. Wander blocked one blow, but the next knocked the sword from Wander's hand. Wander tried to move backward, tried to think of some other weapon, something else that could be used, but the guard was too close now, and the sword was up high—

Then he was falling. Only as he fell did the sounds of connected strikes reach Wander's ears. The blur of motion that was Rucksack paused for just a moment. Behind him, for the first time Wander saw the line of fallen guards, none moving, but as far as Wander could tell, all alive. The fight was putting the fire back into him, thought Wander. For the first time, Wander could see the force, strength, and vitality of the old hero. Wander wondered what it would have been like to see him at the height of his powers.

"Thank you," said Wander.

"You're a survivor," said Rucksack, his face a grim line. "Now survive."

Most of the guards were down now, only two left. Awen and Róisín took one down together. Then Rucksack advanced on the other. Wander realized that they were surrounded—by villagers. The entire village, hundreds of people, had emerged from their huts to watch what was happening. What were they thinking? Would they take up arms if Scáth ordered them to? If they did—

Something caught Wander's eye. The last guard was dead-locked with Rucksack, and they circled each other, sword and staff locked.

Rucksack was losing. His scarred left hand was dropping, and the sword it held back was getting closer and closer to Rucksack's neck. Rucksack was a survivor too—but Wander didn't want to find out if that could include getting his head cut off.

"Rucksack!" yelled Wander. "No!"

Wander ran forward, all thought and fear left behind, no plan, no strategy—only one focus: Protect.

Wander leaned down, gaining speed, and tackled the guard from his left side. The impact made Rucksack stagger. Wander and the guard went to the ground, turning and struggling. Wander grabbed the guard's sword arm and smacked it on the ground again and again, until the hand opened and the sword tumbled away. The guard's other hand swung up and caught Wander on the chin. The guard used the shock to turn them, rolling them so he was on top of Wander, and his hands went around Wander's throat.

Air. There had been air before. Breathing—Wander thought of those last, horrible, ragged breaths that had come from the ragged hut. From Róisín's mother.

And now, from Wander.

Then, from nowhere, a blur came and the last guard fell.

Rucksack swung the staff through, its end cap having whacked the guard hard on the temple. Then he dropped the staff and held out his right hand. Wander took it and got up.

"Thank you again," said Wander. "I've never been much a fighter."

"Never said you were." Rucksack grinned. "I said you were a survivor. And here you are, surviving."

They regrouped with Awen and Róisín.

Then, as one, they turned and looked at Scáth.

He began to yell at the villagers. "Destroy them! Kill them! Tear them to pieces. They are your feast!"

The villagers began to walk toward them. Wander could see it in their eyes: the hunger and the fear, the long, tortured habit of obeying, the terror of the consequences of refusal.

Then Róisín stepped forward. "He murdered my parents," she

yelled. "And he will murder all of us. By degrees. By years. By moments. Do you want to destroy us... or do you want to live? Do you want to be free? If you want to be free, then the time has come. We are not who you seek." Róisín pointed the sword at Scáth. "He is."

No one moved. No one spoke.

Then, as one, the villagers turned and began to walk toward Scáth. Slowly. As if they already knew the outcome.

Scáth turned and ran.

18

______

REBELLION

A crowd of people stood between Scáth and his compound. Fury boiled on his pale, pocked face. Scáth turned in frantic circles, glaring at the people around him. They did not shout or taunt. They did not strike out. They simply stood there, not fighting, but not giving way either.

Wander ran behind Róisín as they pressed through the crowd, Awen and Rucksack close behind. Occasionally Wander could hear a struggle. Other soldiers had been making their way toward the compound. Anytime they did, the otherwise passive people would simply stop them. Outnumbered, Scáth's soldiers were disarmed and restrained. As far as Wander could tell, the fighting was minimal—as, hopefully, were the injuries.

Some of the people held torches, and the flickering fires cast light and shadow around the rough circle the crowd had formed. Whether the light and the darkness were dancing or wrestling, Wander could not decide. The people kept a distance from Scáth, leaving a clear area inside where he scowled and paced like a frustrated beast.

From a scabbard on his belt, he drew a curved knife. "Out of my way," he said. "You have no right to defy me. Out of my way, or

I'll cut you down where you stand. Then I'll cut down the people next to you."

Róisín stepped into the clearing. In the firelight, the blood of her parents glistened on her face. She still held the sword of Destiny, or at least the one Rucksack thought was Destiny. She raised the sword and shouted, "Scáth!"

He turned and looked at her. And grinned.

"You will hurt no one," said Róisín. "Your time of pain and blood and fear has passed."

"Think you can go from worthless dream scum to rebel leader, little one-handed girl?" He spat. "I should have taken your tongue." He chuckled and grinned from the side of his mouth. "Except I thought that once you were grown it would have better uses."

"You took my hand," said Róisín with a slow nod. "You took our freedom. You imprisoned our joy and any love of life. And now you've taken my parents."

"And what will you do now, little rebel?" said Scáth. "Take my life?"

Róisín pulled the sword back toward her, and raised the blade so it pointed upward. "Do you want to die?"

Scáth shrugged. "What is death, and what is life? We're in a dream, little rebel. You'd know that if you knew anything. He has told me. He has shown me. You are not suffering. Your parents are not dead. None of this is real."

"It's real enough for me," said Róisín. "What we choose still matters."

"There is no choice when there is nothing to choose," replied Scáth. "Your parents? I've set them free. They're back somewhere real now. The real place we were all going to go. You never under-stood. None of you. All these years I've tried to show you. Forget about this dream. Follow the real. He was going to take us there, you know. There is a place. A place where there is a wall between this world of dream and the real world beyond. He was going to take us there. His glorious army. We were to destroy the dream—and the dreamer. Then we would become real. You know nothing of life. But we would have. You stupid, stupid girl. Now it's all gone. There's no way he would trust us now."

Róisín smirked. "You offer brutality and murder, and call it a path to glory."

"What will you do different?" He raised his other hand and swept it around the crowd. "See them? They're looking to you now. Ten years, and none have opposed me as you have. Thank goodness you found some strangers to do your dirty work for you."

Rucksack, Awen, and Wander all stood behind Róisín. "Do nothing," whispered Awen.

"He still might kill her," said Wander.

"And she might kill him," replied Awen. "This is her village. If they're going to be free, they'll have to make decisions for themselves."

"So we give them a crash course in justice and vengeance?"

Awen shrugged, but her eyes stayed focused on Róisín—and the other sword stayed in its scabbard on Awen's back. "Let's see what she's learned."

"I can't just stand here," said Wander. "She... She's so young. She's faced so much."

"Just as you did," said Rucksack, his voice gentle. "What happened to you forged you. You couldn't do anything about what happened; you could only do something about what you made of it. Scáth is right about one thing. The people will look to Róisín to lead them. Right now, in this moment, at the point o' that sword, this is where Róisín is going to learn how she will be. How she will lead. What she wants o' herself, o' the people, o' this place and this life. She is deciding her destiny."

"Did Awen give her Destiny, or Decision?"

Rucksack smiled. "We told you we can't tell them apart."

Róisín took a few steps toward Scáth. The sword was relaxed

yet ready, and Wander realized how surprisingly calm the woman was. All that pain. All that grief. It forged a person, reshaped them. Right now, that process was going on before their eyes. But what, thought Wander, was it making of Róisín?

"I have every right to kill you," said Róisín. "Execute you for all you've done against us. Against me. You have caused uncountable death and immeasurable suffering. You have taken this from a place of happiness to a place of terror."

Scáth took a few steps toward her. "Stupid girl," he said. "You talk too much."

He dashed forward, knife pointed toward Róisín.

There, in that moment, the paths of the future shone. One dark but getting brighter. The other tinged and saturated with blood. In that moment, the world seemed to slow down.

Wander wanted to look away but kept watching. This was it. Róisín could make one simple slash, and take a hand for a hand. The katana had a far superior reach than the knife, even Wander could see that. The curved blade was far sharper than the rough knife Scáth was now stabbing toward Róisín. And Róisín did have every right. He had cut off her hand when she was a child—why not return the favor? And maybe hack off a few more bits for good measure, like collecting interest on a very, very old debt.

Or Róisín could swing a little differently and stab Scáth through the heart, or take off his arm at the shoulder, or plunge the sword through Scáth's neck. All would harm him, end him, and maybe, just maybe, start to balance the scales.

But if it turned Róisín into someone who could kill easily, what did that do to the balance?

How would she lead, if she knew how easily one could turn to bloodshed?

The knife was almost to Róisín now.

Wander felt a pressure—Rucksack had taken Wander's hand. Wander squeezed back. The terror and tension Wander felt,

Rucksack clearly felt too, and Wander understood how hard it was for him not to intervene—how hard, but also how essential.

The things that had happened to Róisín, to her people, to her village, she could not control.

But what she did with it, in this moment—she could.

The point of the knife would split the skin, drive through the bone, and eat her heart. She would be dead in an instant. A brilliant young woman who had lost so much, now would lose her life.

Scáth put all his weight behind the blow. So much faster than Wander would have thought possible, Róisín moved. She pivoted on one foot, turning her body so she was now off to one side, out of the path of the knife.

Scáth's momentum made him keep lunging forward, but the evasion surprised him and took him off balance. He tried to slash backward and off to the side, but Róisín danced around behind him, to the side where there was no knife.

Now she raised the katana. Over her head, hand strong around the grip.

Róisín chose.

She brought the sword's end cap, pointing out from under the bottom of her fist, down hard on the back of Scáth's neck, right at the base of his skull.

He crumpled, still conscious, but dazed and weakened. When he hit the ground, the knife bounced out of his hand. Wander kicked it away, toward Awen, and Awen picked it up.

On all fours, Scáth raised himself to his knees. He locked his gaze on Róisín. His eyes were completely black.

"Fine," he said. "Fine. I'm done being in this damn dream anyway. Go ahead, then, little rebel. You've got the big bad sword. I tried to kill you. There is only one fate for me. You want to lead? Then you have to make the hard choices. They'll be expecting you too. That's what it means, to have the big compound, to have the responsibility, to know the glorious destiny that you vermin must be prepared to meet. I've tried. I've failed him, but he will forgive me. One day I will meet him in the dream, and he will take my hand, and I will lead him to the wall itself. So go ahead, little rebel. You take it all over. Kill me. Róisín, kill me."

Wander thought Róisín had chosen. But nothing could be decided, nothing could be certain, while Scáth lived.

Smiling, Róisín set the point of the sword against Scáth's throat.

19

DROP

"This is the moment, isn't it?" said Róisín. In the deep night only the torches glowed, but it was more than enough for Wander to see the absolute fury, the righteous indignation, the perfect rage that blazed in Róisín's eyes and on her face.

Róisín pressed the tip of Destiny into the bump at Scáth's voice box, just enough to draw the tiniest drop of blood. A little rivulet flowed down his throat and spent itself in the rough fabric of his shirt. Wander thought of the flood that was about to follow.

"Please, Róisín, no," said Wander. "Don't do this."

"Don't interfere." Rucksack grabbed Wander's wrist. "She must make her choices. It's not our right to tell her who she is."

"I'm not interfering," replied Wander sharply. "I'm reminding her of exactly that—it's her choice. Justice. Vengeance. She in this moment is the one deciding that. So yes, I'll make damn sure she knows it. And if you don't like it, then you can go to hell. Or whatever passes for hell here."

In the flickering torchlight, it was hard to read the fallen hero's face. But Wander was certain that he gave a nod, and that maybe, just maybe, one corner of his mouth twitched upward in a grin. Either way, he let go of Wander's wrist. Wander walked over toward Róisín. Scáth looked from Róisín to Wander, and back to Róisín.

"Ah, the voice of conscience," he said.

"I won't have this moment decided for me," said Róisín.

"I wouldn't dream of trying to decide it for you," replied Wander. "Neither would anyone else." And no one did. All the villagers stood in their silent circle, watching Róisín. Wander tried to read their faces, read their gazes, but everything was so dark. Wander could not tell what they wished for, what they burned for, right now.

"He has killed so many. My parents just happened to be the last people he got to torment and murder." Róisín's sword arm tensed, as if readying for the final thrust forward. "And I just happen to be holding the sword. It could have been any of the others."

Wander nodded. "It could have been, but it wasn't. It was you. Destiny, decision, choice, circumstance—I don't give a damn what anyone calls it. The simple fact of the matter is that you are the one here. In this moment. At this crossroads. I've had my own pain, but I cannot possibly imagine what you are going through. What you have gone through. I won't try to dissuade you. But for what it's worth, I will tell you this: There's been enough killing. Ten years of death and pain. Taking his life won't give you back your hand, or bring back your parents, or return the dead to the living. It won't dry tears or calm nightmares."

"No," said Róisín. "It won't. But him no longer being among the living certainly will bring a few smiles."

Róisín turned her body, and her gaze pinned Scáth's. She pressed the point of the sword. A little more blood flowed, pooling in the hollow of his throat. Scáth's eyes widened, but otherwise he showed no feeling, no pain.

"His life is mine by right," said Róisín. "I'm going to claim it now."

20

JUSTICE SERVED

Róisín lowered the sword.

The villagers surrounding them looked to one another in confusion. Murmurs went around the crowd.

"What are you doing?" said Scáth. "Kill me. At least if I'm dead I won't have to listen to you anymore." A spark of panic flared into his voice. "You said you were going to kill me!"

"I said I was going to claim your life," replied Róisín softly. "I never said I would kill you. For ten years we've known nothing but bloodshed, fear, death, and the threat of death. When death is so much a part of your life, killing should be easy. You're a disease. A rot that should be cut away from the body of this place."

"Then do it." He shuffled forward on his knees, toward the lowered sword, like a dog seeking its master.

"I won't be like you," said Róisín. "Killing you would start me down a path that I choose not to follow."

Róisín stuck the sword into the ground. She looked at the villagers. "I spare his life," she said, "but Scáth is no more."

"You are a coward," said Scáth. "You dare to spare me? You're just too weak to kill me."

"No," said Róisín. "You deserve to die, but you're going to be too busy."

"What are you talking about?" spat Scáth.

Róisín ignored him, addressing the surrounding villagers. "I am not sparing Scáth's life because I fear killing him. And not even because I fear becoming like him, though I would avoid it." Róisín looked from person to person, a light flaring in her eyes. "I have a question for you. The fall of Scáth leaves us in need of leadership. Who would you have lead us?"

Wander had gone back to Rucksack and Awen. They looked around the crowd but stayed silent.

After silent moments, a voice went up. "We would have you lead us, Róisín."

Someone nodded. Someone said, "Aye!" More assents came, and soon the entire village was calling for Róisín to lead them.

"Then I'll accept. It's with a heavy, grieving heart," she said, "but I will lead as best I can. And I thank you for this trust. We will know light and laughter, music and community again. We will return to our name."

Then Róisín said a word, a single word.

"Shantermon."

At the sound of the three syllables, all the villagers went silent. Many began to weep. They all began to repeat the word, over and over, as if hearing it for the first time.

"Shantermon," said Róisín. "Before she died, my mother remembered. On her dying breath, she whispered our village's name to me. As she returned it to me, now I return it to all of you."

Rucksack nodded. "Old Refuge. May it be so again."

Old Refuge was a literal translation, but Wander knew what the long-forgotten name really meant: home.

Róisín stood next to the sword, but she did not take it up again. "As the leader of Shantermon, I now must decide the fate of Scáth. I will tell you what I believe my decision to be, but it is up to you whether or not to accept it. You have also known loss. You have also known death and grief and torment. If you wish me to kill him, then I will. But here is what I suggest we do instead."

Róisín smiled, and she stared hard at Scáth. "I sentence you," she said, "to a lifetime of helping. You must aid the village in all its many needs. You will tend to the hurt, the hungry, the sick, the old. You will mend them when they need mending. You will help in the building of new housing and in the planting of new fields. Of course, I trust you about as much as you trust me, so you will do this in shackles and under guard. I'd hate for you to think you could leave this fine village, which you've invested so much time and work in."

Murmurs went around the villagers: questions, debate.

"I am to be your slave, then?" said Scáth.

Róisín raised her hand, and all fell silent. "Not a slave. A servant," she said. "And not my servant. The village's. But far more than that. You will listen. You will work side by side with the people here, and you will hear their tales. You will hear all they are willing to tell. Every story of death and heartache, of starvation and suffering. You will know their stories as your own. You will understand what they have gone through, what they have lost because of you. You will hear and feel all the pain that you have caused. Every day. For the rest of your life. That is your sentence." Róisín looked at the villagers. "Do you agree?"

The villagers began to talk, quietly at first, then more loudly as they realized they could at last speak freely. Then, after much discussion, the voices settled and all looked at Róisín. "Aye," they said together. "It is just."

Róisín looked at Scáth. "So be it," she said. "What you have done wrong, you will spend your remaining life putting right."

"Every day listening to their pain?" said Scáth. "Toiling in the muck and the mud, and hearing them prattle on because of what I did or caused?" He stood and yelled at the crowd. "I could have made you an army! You have no idea what is really going on.

What you really are. What we could have been!" He turned and looked at Róisín. "I'll tell you what I think of your sentence, you disgusting child. What I think of your village."

He thrust his hand into his shirt and drew a knife.

Rucksack started to reach for his sword, but Awen stopped him. "Wait," she said.

Scáth chuckled and pointed the knife toward Róisín. "I am just a dream. You are just a dream. But the shadow is real." He smiled. "What happens to me doesn't matter. The shadow will swallow you in its darkness. I'll be waiting for you there."

Scáth turned the knife and plunged it into his heart.

He sank back to his knees, and his dark eyes faded. Then Scáth, the shadow of the shadow, fell face down to the ground and was no more.

Róisín shrugged. "Well," she said, "that'll work too."

Around them, Wander realized, the first brightening of daybreak had begun. The people of Shantermon began to come forward, many to talk with Róisín, or Wander, or Awen, or Rucksack. People shared their names as if sharing precious treasures—ones they were finding again after years of fearing they were lost. The sun rose in the Irish morning, warm and bright in a clear sky.

People went into the compound that Scáth had occupied, and broke open his massive stores of food. The soldiers who had guarded Scáth were all given a similar choice: They could help, or they could die. Either would do.

The villagers carried Scáth's body from the village. In a spot near some trees, they buried him. Before they covered him with earth, one of the villagers, an older woman, set an acorn on the bloody patch over his heart.

Seeing Róisín taking a break from setting out large tables, Wander and Awen came over to the young leader. Her face looked young, but Wander could see how her eyes had changed—still bright, but carrying a sadness that would never leave.

"I have to ask," said Wander. "Why didn't you just kill him?"

"It would have been natural, and I had every right," said Róisín. "But him and people like him... all they have is pain, fear, and death. They have no tools, only weapons. I chose to offer him redemption because that was the only way we ourselves could change too. Whether or not he accepted was up to him. But I had to offer it, lest I find myself one day needing it."

Wander looked at Awen. "Why didn't you do more? Aren't you supposed to be the light, the guide?"

"The purpose of the light is to shine," replied Awen. "But I told you, I'm a mirror too. To shine is to help others find the light in themselves, to help them find their own way. As for doing more... what makes you think I didn't do what needed to be done?"

Wander could think of no reply.

Throughout the day the villagers talked and worked. People began pulling vegetables, fruit, meat, cheese, and flour from the compound. Along with, it turned out, many secret kegs of Galway Pradesh Stout.

That evening, as the sun set on the village's first free day, Róisín raised a goblet. "To freedom," she said. "To us."

They drank, and Róisín added, "And to new friends." She looked at Rucksack, Awen, and Wander, who sat near her at the table. "You took a chance. You helped people you did not know, risking your lives. We will always be in your debt, and we hope that we will always be counted as your friends. You will always be welcome in Shantermon. Know that wherever you roam, you may always count this as home."

They all drank to the toast. And for some days after, the trio stayed in the village, helping where they could help, and giving council to Róisín as she settled in to her new role. Then, when the day was right, Wander, Awen, and Rucksack rose early. Róisín walked with them as they left Shantermon. They said their good-byes. And then, as Róisín watched them leave, Rucksack, Awen, and Wander returned to the Black Road.

21

WANDER'S FAVORITE PLACE

As it had when they first set foot on the Black Road, the morning light faded. Sounds muted. All the world fell away, except for the mile-wide expanse of char and ash.

"You're quiet this morning," said Rucksack.

"Was thinking about everything that happened," said Wander. "All the years I've been on the road, alone, no friendships, no relationships. The occasional fling. There have been people along the way I've felt close to, but then I move on or they move on. Now here I am, in this weird world, and so much has happened just in a few days."

"It's a lot to take in."

"Something feels different," said Wander, "but I don't know what it is yet."

"It's not what's happened to you," added Awen. "Is it who you're with?"

Wander grinned. "That would be some of it. The ancient hero and the light of Ireland. You certainly make for interesting companions. But more than that... we are walking this strange road together. We were captured and held prisoner together... We fought together... Together... Together we helped a lot of people.

Nothing like that has ever happened to me." Wander looked at Rucksack. "No one like you has ever happened to me."

"Perhaps this world isn't such a bad place for you after all," replied Rucksack.

"Journeys and challenges forge strong bonds," said Awen.

They walked a while in silence, each step taking them closer and closer to Galway, closer and closer to where The Blast had happened, to where Rucksack had been so injured, to where they would have to make him relive what had happened. Wander felt both an ease and a tension, and both intensified each time Wander looked at Rucksack. He had been so hurt, and he was still so lost and scared, but he was still fighting, still trying, still seeking his place in the world, his redemption and his destiny. But beyond that, he was kind. The time in Shantermon had shown Wander a bit of Rucksack's heart.

Yet a tension sprung up in Wander too, for the village had also shown Rucksack some of Wander's heart.

"What you did there, in the village," said Rucksack, "it was impressive."

"I'm no fighter," said Wander. "And I don't really want to be."

"That's not what I mean," he said. "You knew what needed to be done, and you did it. All my years wandering this world, and it still amazes me how rarely that happens."

Wander chuckled. "You could say the same thing about my world."

"Had you not been here, things could have been very different."

"Had you not been here," said Awen, "we still may not have known about Shantermon. Scáth may indeed have succeeded in what he was trying to do. Even if we had bested him, I don't know if Róisín would have made the same choice."

"I'm no warrior," said Wander, "but talking to her was something I was capable of doing. Something I had to do. Staying silent would have been as wrong as running away."

"You talked mercy to an angry person who had every right to kill someone and was holding a powerful sword," said Rucksack. "That alone takes more than a share o' courage."

"I just did what needed to be done."

Awen patted Wander's arm. "And that, my dear, is what was so right. Things turned out the way they did because of you."

Wander's cheeks flushed. "Thank you."

As they neared Galway, Wander noticed the gaiety in Rucksack's face fading and fading, as if the village hadn't happened.

"I went there," said Wander, "in my world. Galway. Spent a lot of time there. Thought about spending more. I'd been plenty of places at that point, but nothing stuck with me like Galway did. I loved that city. The beer, the music, the bay, the cobblestone streets. I... I actually thought about moving there. Maybe settling down for a little while. Work in a shop or a pub or something. After the tornado took my home and family, I'd never felt a desire to stay anywhere. But I did in Galway."

Awen said nothing. Neither did Rucksack.

"Guys?" said Wander. "Sorry... I... maybe I overshared... Thought we, you know, were getting closer. Thought, well, since we were getting close, and Galway matters so much to both of you, well, you know, it was, I don't know, worth talking about."

The others still said nothing, but a grave, pained look passed between Awen and Rucksack.

The Black Road took them to the bottom of a charred and blackened hill. "At the top," said Awen, her voice thin, as if she were in pain, "we'll be able to see all of Galway."

They went up the hill, Awen in front, Rucksack in the rear. Wander would peek back at him now and again. Each time he seemed paler, his lips in a tight line. Sometimes he clenched and unclenched his left hand.

"Are you okay?" said Wander. "You seem like you're in pain."

"I'm terrified," said Rucksack. "And I am in pain. Just being here... my hand is throbbing." He looked away. "If only that were the worst o' it."

They neared the top of the hill, and Awen paused. "Rucksack," she said, her voice gentle. "You knew we had to come here."

"I knew the road led here," he said. "I didn't know it would hurt this much. Let's just get there, Awen. The sooner this is over, the better."

Wander looked back and forth between them. "You said The Blast was terrible—I get that," said Wander. "What aren't you telling me?"

"Only what can't be told," said Awen, sadness in her eyes. "What must be shown."

They came to the top of the hill. And Wander saw.

"This can't be Galway," said Wander. "This is just an ash heap."

"Nowadays we call it Galway Ruin," said Awen softly. "The Blast didn't just happen in the vicinity. This city was the very epicenter. Galway is gone. Ash is all that's left."

Wander gasped. Memories came back. Crowds in the city center. People walking along the bay. The pubs at night, full of beer, laughter, and music. The Galway of Wander's world, yes, but it would have been much like the Galway of this world too. "It can't be."

"No matter how much pain it comes with," said Awen, "your heart knows the truth." Weariness weighed down the older woman's voice and body.

Wander looked away. "Why didn't you tell me?"

"You loved it so much," said Awen, her voice gentle. "We didn't have the heart to tell you yet."

"And it's not really something that can be easily told," added Rucksack. "Something like this... the scope o' it only makes sense when you see it for yourself."

Wander had gotten used to the Black Road, to the wide expanse of charred, lifeless nothing. It was horrible, but Wander had always found a comfort in silence.

But it was nothing compared to Galway Ruin.

The blackness fanned out as far as Wander could see. No buildings. No trees. No life. All was a flat plain of ash and char, all black and gray, as if a shadow had fallen over the world. The only change in the landscape was from hills, but those, too, were as blackened and charred as where Wander stood.

"I'm glad that in your world there is still a Galway, and that it is still a beautiful place," said Rucksack. "But here, in this one, all was lost. Because o' me. Because I failed."

"And that's why we have to be here, Rucksack," said Awen. "I've tried to ease you into this as best I could. But there's too much happening, and the village proved that things are worse than I feared."

"I don't know if I can do this, Awen."

She shrugged. "If you want to help Wander, if you want to help yourself, if you want to help the world, you're going to have to remember it. No, not remember it. Relive it. The Blast itself didn't kill you. I don't think reliving it will, either."

"Maybe it just has to finish me off," said Rucksack.

"Then you aren't much of a hero after all," said Awen.

Wander's eyes widened. The guide and the fallen hero glared at each other, until Rucksack looked away.

"You know where we must go," said Awen. "All the way down. All the way through. To the epicenter. To where The Blast happened."

Rucksack nodded but said nothing.

They made their way down the hill, no longer together, it seemed to Wander, but just three people who happened to be going the same way. For now.

22

———

REMEMBER

Rucksack looked around, then stopped. "This is it." His voice was barely a whisper. Tears flooded his dark eyes. He fell to his knees and said nothing else.

Wander choked back vomit. The silence here, the chill in the air. The Black Road had been eerie, but this, this was sickening. Every breath was somehow foul, as if they were in a slaughter-house or a cemetery.

And that was the thing, Wander realized.

They were.

All around them, death. Ash like black pepper, but that was the least troubling aspect. Ash was abstract. Proof of burning, but no sense of what had burned. Among the ash was fragments. Bones. Warped metalwork like tools and hinges. Half-molten toys and dolls. The ash they stood on—buildings and roads, but also people, pets, livestock. A city of tens of thousands. All gone.

The sky had turned gray, and the view began to shorten and shrink. Fog came over Galway Ruin. Soon they could hardly see each other.

"Stay close," said Awen. "Stay together." She stood in front of Rucksack and got down on her knees.

"It's time," said Awen. "Tell us everything. My friend. Faddah Rucksack." She touched his face. "Please."

"What could we possibly gain?" said Rucksack. His voice was weak, and his rich dark skin had paled so much he looked albino.

"We can gain understanding," replied Awen. "What happened then may matter to what happens now. Above all, you can drain this wound. Not your hand. But the hurt inside. The damage to your spirit."

"I failed, Awen, that's all that matters. That's all that will ever matter."

"Only as long as you let it." Awen leaned back and stood. "Besides," she said, "you can hardly stand right now, and we're not leaving until you've told us. So if you want to leave, then talk."

Rucksack nodded. Awen helped him to his feet. "Wander," she said, "take my hand and Rucksack's."

"I still hate this idea, Awen," said Rucksack.

"So do I," said Awen. "If you have a better option, I'd love to hear it."

"What exactly are we going to do?" said Wander.

"This is not a story that can be told as if we were sitting around a campfire having a beer," said Awen. "This is a story that must be lived."

"So you're telling me that we're going to go, what, into Rucksack's memory?"

"Precisely."

Rucksack started to repeat his objection, but Wander squeezed his hand. The world seemed to spin, and all went dark.

Then Wander could see again.

23

RUCKSACK'S FAILURE

The world was a gray sky, damp earth covered in green. Mist hung in the air. Nearby, the city of Galway bustled, and the sounds of life reached the small, green, grassy hill just outside the city. There were no candles, no torches. It was daytime, yet dim as dusk. In the sky above Faddah Rucksack, between him and the low dark clouds, a small orb glowed.

Rucksack stared at the impossible star. It alternated between glowing with a brilliant white light and then went as dark as the deepest shadows. He tried to understand. What was this? Why was it here? And why was it above him?

A slight breeze ruffled the orange silk of his shirt and pants. He tugged on the black sash around his waist. Two swords were strapped to his back. And he understood. He remembered. This day. This terrible day. The day had begun so bright. His mother and father had asked him to take care. They were worried about him, but he did not understand why. He was more powerful than ever. He had righted so many wrongs. They had begun to wonder if this day would ever come.

Now it had come: the day of his destiny.

All these long, long years, Rucksack had fought for the world, his unchanging face a constant through all threats, conflicts, and turmoil. Fought for life. Protected. Inspired. He only fought when he had to, and he did anything he could to prevent a fight. No ultimate good ever came from having a bigger fist or a harder punch. Rucksack had spent his whole life, all ten thousand years, trying to live up to that. Protect the world, but in a way that honored what was being protected. Inspire the world by being someone others could aspire to be like.

Now here it was. The moment of realization and of reward. The destiny he had waited for, fought for, strived for, loved for, sacrificed for.

Ready. For him.

The small star hung below the clouds, gently pulsating, shimmering from gold to silver, then to black, and back to gold.

"For Mother and Father," he said. "For all who have come before. For all who live now. For all who are to come. For the world as it was, the world as it is, the world as it could be." He stood tall and raised his hands toward the star.

Then he saw them. Coming over the small rise, first his mother and then his father came into view.

"Are you sure you're ready?" said his mother.

"I was born for this. So many times I have nearly died for this. And now, for this I live," Rucksack replied.

"Son, be sure this is what you want," said his father. "Anything can happen. You know that. Everything will change—but ultimately, what changes is what also stays the same. Who you are, who you ultimately are, at your heart, at your soul—that will come out so that it is all that you can live, all that you can be. Are you sure you're ready for this?"

Rucksack nodded. "It's time, Father. For so long we have strived. Wandered. Made a life for ourselves. We have fought and fled. We have given up so much. Now it is time to gain all and give all."

"Once the *dia ubh* opens, son, the god egg will change everything," said his mother. "Stand in that light, and all will be revealed. Who you are. Who you will be."

"As it should be," said Rucksack. "I'm ready. You're ready. And the world is ready too. There is much we have done."

"Much you have done," said his mother.

Rucksack shrugged. "There is much still to be done. This needs to happen. The things that need to happen in the world... the understanding people need—think of what will happen soon. We can see it now. Across the ocean, a country will split in two, and blood will pour from north to south. Here where we stand, the very ground will seem to rot, and millions will starve. That is but the beginning o' the horrors we have seen in the future's dreaming shadows. Is there to be hope? Is there to be help? If so, then this is the hour o' my destiny. This is the moment I will become what I must be. Hero o' old. Hero o' now. Hero o' always. But only if this comes to pass."

His mother and father nodded, but there seemed to be a sadness in their eyes, a doubt. Maybe just anxiety. Maybe something else, but Rucksack could not ask what it was. Not now. Now, when all was so close.

The star's pulsating changed, then stopped. Rucksack held his breath, wondering what was next.

The dia ubh split in two.

Now a gold orb glowed above him, but nearby, to the left of the first, a black orb spun too.

"Why are there two?" he asked.

"It is said that there are always two," said his mother. "Destiny is a crossroads. When you stand here, in the path of the opening dia ubh, there is a path of light and a path of dark. When you stand in the power of the dia ubh, we will soon know which path you are on."

Rucksack looked at his mother. "Do you doubt which?"

She did not answer.

The two orbs spun faster and faster. The air became calm,

eerily charged, as if a tornado were about to come to earth. But it was only the gathering of the power, the impossible vastness of power that would pour forth from the dia ubh. The power to change what needed to be changed—and the power to know what should be changed. The power to change a person into a god.

The two orbs recombined.

"It is time," said Rucksack. "Whoever I become, I still am me. I love you, Father. I love you, Mother. All will be well." He smiled. "At last."

He prepared for the small star to split, for its golden light to pour down over him.

Then, just as he stared at the star, its light dimmed. A shadow passed over the star.

"No!" yelled Rucksack. The darkness was there—he could see it all over the surface of the star now.

A man was flying over the dia ubh, then coming toward it.

Rucksack knew the man had to be stopped, but everything was happening fast now—

At the edges of his vision, Rucksack could see the terrified expressions frozen on the faces of his parents. The dia ubh flashed gold and silver, then black—not only black, but darkness beyond any Rucksack had ever seen. Darker than nights without stars or moon. Darker than the deepest caves he had roamed. Darker than the worst fears that now were coming true before his eyes.

The dia ubh flashed gold and silver again. The brilliance stayed. Maybe it would be okay after all. The brightness was there again, the brilliance like the sun.

Then black.

Then black and gold, swirling and shining, threaded and entwined.

The shadow became the dia ubh.

The flying man was doing something to the dia ubh. Rucksack thought no more. He knew only that he must meet this shadow, this villain, in midair, and stop what was happening. The roar of the tiger filled the air. Rucksack's feet left the ground. The balance was being destroyed. If the balance of the dia ubh, the light and the dark, was destroyed, then Rucksack feared for what would happen next.

The dia ubh stopped swirling. The gold and black froze.

Then they burned.

The shadow was still. Rucksack was close, but still too far away, too far—

"It can't be like this!" shouted Rucksack's father. It was the last time Rucksack heard his father speak.

The dia ubh turned gray. Then it bloomed into orange and black, opening petals of fire upon the world.

Rucksack heard his mother cry out—for him, for the world, for his father—and then she was silent.

Rucksack heard his own cries, but only for the barest moment. The dia ubh ripped open, broken and torn by the unknown shadow.

Tendrils of fire spread north, east, south, and west. All around, everything the fire touched burst into flame.

"Galway!" Rucksack cried. "Mother! Father! I'm sorry!"

Then he too was burning, and no longer flying but falling, and all the world was orange and nothing and black.

24

VOICE

Awen, Rucksack, and Wander had all fallen down, and the ash crunched as they began to get back up. At least, Awen and Wander were rising. Rucksack was trying, but he kept falling over.

Wander moved to him. "Rucksack! Rucksack!"

"I can feel it all again," he said. "Had to make it stop... there was nothing else there, nothing else—"

"You heard Awen," said Wander. "You have to—"

"Not for me," he said, tears now running down his face. "For you. Both of you. The burning. The death. The screams. The loss. The holes in the world. The torn destinies o' so many people... I feel it, Wander. I'm living each one. Every person. Every life. I feel it all. I have ever since The Blast happened, and I have ever since I woke up. It's like I'm still burning, Wander. Like the world is still burning. I feel this every moment. I was reborn in fire, and I relive that fire with every breath. It's bad enough that I feel it. I couldn't let you and Awen feel it too."

He fell over, face crunching in the ash.

"Rucksack?" said Awen. "Get up. You have to get up."

"It's this damn place," said Wander. "We've got to get him out of here. Off the char. Off the Black Road. It burns at him far worse than it does us."

"We leave this, we're vulnerable."

"For all we can tell, this is killing him," said Wander. "If we stay here, then him surviving might be short-lived. It'll be like The Blast just waited to finish the job."

Awen said nothing, just helped pull up Rucksack while Wander did the same. Together they half-dragged, half-carried him down the hill, across the ash and char and darkness.

The world was black and gray, just the ash and the fog, and Wander began to think they would never see light again, or a blue sky, or even a cloudy one. There was nothing here, just the shadow they walked on and the gray dimness they trudged through.

Then, ahead, a slash of green.

Awen pulled them forward. Wander's every muscle burned and wanted to collapse, but Wander kept moving. If they stayed, the burning would never stop.

The gray vanished. Sunlight returned to the world, and the sky was blue around a bright sun lowering in the western sky.

And they stood on grass.

Breathing hard, muscles giving in, all three collapsed onto the grass. The little blades tickled Wander's nose, and it was glorious.

Lying there, Wander stared at the sky and the sun and tried to love them. But all Wander could see was that impossible star in that impossible sky. Wander looked over at Rucksack, who was still unconscious.

"Darkness and flame, that's what you see," said Wander. "That's what you relive at every moment." Something in Wander's heart reached for him, and Wander squeezed his hand.

Then the voice came.

"Hello?" it said in a tone golden and lovely, educated and radiant. "Are you okay?"

Awen sat up.

A beautiful woman walked toward them.

25

HELP

"I was out for a walk and heard your cries." The woman moved toward them quickly, with a solid grace, her frame neither bulky nor petite. Over a creamy-white shirt, her reddish-brown open vest and matching pants rustled slightly. "You must need help." She brushed a long golden lock of hair from her slender face, then she touched Awen's face and looked deep into the older woman's eyes. "You look so tired," said the woman.

"Our friend is sick," said Awen.

"He sometimes has... episodes," added Wander.

The woman kneeled down and began to look at Rucksack. She touched his face, the same way she did Awen's. "You poor dears," she said. "It's going to be okay. Fiach will tend to you."

A fresh wail from Rucksack split the air, and Wander stumbled backward a couple of steps.

"No!" he shouted. "No!"

"It's going to be okay," said Wander. "We have help. This person can help you."

"No!" he shouted again, trying to struggle up from the ground. "She's... She's not... here... to..."

Fiach kicked him in the face. The back of Rucksack's head

smacked the earth and he lay still. She leaped forward and grabbed Wander's face. Behind Fiach, Awen quickly lunged. Without looking away, Fiach swung back a fist into Awen's temple. The older woman collapsed.

Fiach clasped both hands on Wander's face. Wander yelled. The hands burned, but there was something else, something—

Fiach's eyes widened, and she did not let go. "Of course," said Fiach. "Of course it's you. The scent is so powerful, I could have smelled you from Rome, but England sufficed. But up close... up close it's so powerful, it's so mesmerizing... It takes over everything. I couldn't tell for sure until I touched you. But now I have. Now I know. And he'll know too. You'll come with me."

Wander knocked away the woman's hands. "No thanks. You're not the kind of stranger I like to talk to."

"You don't need to talk. You just need to obey. All is easier when you do. With me. And with him too."

"Who?" said Wander. "The shadow?"

Fiach laughed. "Is that what these fools call him? He would no doubt find your male friend amusing. And the old woman... such a fanciful name. He will lead the world out of darkness, out of dream, and into the light of true reality. He will teach us, if only we are willing to learn. He will leave his mark. He is not the shadow. He is the guru."

Fiach leaned away. Wander could see a raw red mark, an inch thick, wrapped around Fiach's throat like a collar.

"Did this guru give you that?" said Wander. "That's a messed-up lesson."

Fiach shrugged. "I disobeyed, and obedience is everything. The only way out of the dream is to follow one who is awake. I did not listen, and I had to be reminded of my role, my path. I remember now." She smiled, but the sharpness in her green eyes made Wander take a step back. "I will not need to be reminded ever again. In time, you won't either. Now come on. It will be easier. The guru wants to hear all about the fascinating world you must be from."

Wander's mouth fell open. "How could you possibly know that?"

"A soul forged in another world. No wonder he needs you. You are the key to everything. You are the answer to the question he never stops asking. He has sought and sought a key like you." Fiach smiled so big now, Wander worried her face would split. "He will be so happy I found you. You will unlock the worlds, little other-soul. You will be his key. Then the guru can take all that is wrong, which is everything, and make it right. Let's go now. Leave these others to their dreams a little longer. Maybe those are better than the fake life they're living now."

"You must be right," said Wander. "I'm not from here after all. What do I know? This guru guy makes a lot of sense. These two just happened to be the first people I came across anyway. What do they know?"

Fiach cocked her head, and Wander began walking that way, slightly in front. "I heard a story about you," said Wander. "A guy, recently, some story about a hound that scented out and hunted souls. Souls that were different. Never would have thought he was talking about you. But I guess it makes sense."

"What makes sense?"

"That you'd be talked about like a dog." Wander took a step, paused. "You're certainly a..."

Wander lunged around to catch Fiach off guard. Fiach, though, simply knocked Wander away. Wander hit the ground hard, panting and wheezing. Fiach drew back her foot to kick at Wander's head. Wander tried to move, get up, get away, but couldn't, couldn't, and now the foot was flying—

Fiach was gone. Muffled thumps and shouts rolled along the ground. Wander fought to get breath back, then slowly stood.

Rucksack was on top of Fiach, punching her and punching her.

Fiach fought back too though, and soon they were apart, eyeing each other, circling, the tiger and the hound.

"Wander is under my protection," said Rucksack. "As are this world and all in it. Tell that to your feckin guru when you get back to him, with your tail between your legs."

"You are fascinating," said Fiach. "You smell so familiar yet so strange. I can't place it. But I am only here for the soul from another world. You are in the way, though." She smiled again. "I am allowed to kill whatever is in my way."

"You're welcome to try."

Fiach lunged. Roars and growls filled Wander's ears. Fiach and Rucksack were blurs too fast for Wander to follow. Wander had seen it in him in Shantermon, regaining his strength, his power coming back, his confidence, but this—he had been out cold, and now it was as if he were fighting for the most important thing in the world.

Rucksack took a step back. So did Fiach. They came together again—but as Rucksack moved, Fiach grabbed his left hand just so, and he roared with pain and fell over. Fiach picked up a large rock and held it high over her head. The rock came down toward Rucksack's skull.

Awen's stick flashed and the rock flew aside. Fiach looked up, but too late, and Awen was on her now. Even after seeing Awen fight in the village, the older woman was faster and stronger than Wander had realized. Every time Fiach moved, Awen seemed to already be where Fiach was heading. The stick flashed again—and Fiach was on the ground.

And did not get up.

"Is she dead?" asked Wander as the three of them came together again.

"Not at the moment," replied Awen, a coldness in her voice that Wander had not heard before.

"Are you suggesting you're going to change that?" said Rucksack.

Awen raised the point of the stick over Fiach's temple. She tensed, and started to pull up, then—

"Please don't kill her," said Wander.

Awen shook her head and stared hard at Wander. "Not a line I plan to cross. I'm just irked that she got me by surprise, and with such a cheap shot. But you speak with such compassion in your voice. She is here for you. Perhaps to kill you, or have you killed, which really amounts to the same thing. Why plead for her life?"

The force of it hit Wander. It was dizzying, all the pain and loneliness. The world's colors ran like paint diluting in water. Rucksack held onto Wander, providing stability, and the world became solid again.

"It happened when she touched my face," said Wander. "Whatever she was feeling for in us, she found it in me... It worked both ways, though I don't think she knew that. She could sense me. My life. Where I'm from. She knows. But I could also sense her. I could see her memories. Her heart. She was made like this. Orphaned by fire when she was a little girl, and taken in by this guru. Twisted and tormented. Raised not like a person, but like a dog. She really is like a hound, only in human form. She's been mistreated and abused beyond belief."

"By this guru?" said Rucksack.

"By him," said Wander. "He's the shadow, Awen. Only she doesn't call him that. She says he's a guru. A teacher. She talked of Guru, as if it were his name."

"You're saying you could see into her mind?"

Wander nodded. "Not very pleasant, believe me. She... She did not choose this. Choice was taken from her. She told me obedience was everything. That's all she knows. She is here because this guru told her to come, and she would not dream of anything but obeying his every wish."

"What do you propose?" said Rucksack. "We can't just leave her here."

Wander walked around, trying to think of a solution. A little ways away from where they had first spotted Fiach, Wander found a small leather backpack. Inside was the answer. Wander came back. "This was likely meant for me," said Wander, unwinding a long black rope that had been coiled inside the pack. "So let's return the favor."

Wander unwound the long black rope. Soon they had tied up Fiach. They left some food and water from the pack near the unconscious woman, then they quickly made their way back to the Black Road.

Wander's eyes closed a moment, then Wander heard the familiar crunch of ash under boots again.

The sun faded and the sky turned gray. Sound left the world, along with color, happiness, and hope.

"I hate being here," said Wander.

"Of course you do," said Awen. "You're alive. You don't believe that misery is our natural state. You recognize this place as a sign of great wrong, a wound that may never heal."

"It will never go back?" said Wander. "Even a place ravaged by a volcano blast can one day come back."

"This is different," said Awen. "Galway Ruin will never be inhabited again. Nothing grows. All is black and always will be black."

"But London came back after The Blast," said Wander.

"London was lucky," said Awen. "On the Black Road, it's the only place that has defied the ruin. But this place will always be a ruin. The Black Cliffs will never turn white again, my friend. All is ruin here. And that, I'm afraid, is our road."

"Fiach will get out, won't she?" said Wander.

"O' course she will," said Rucksack. "But whether or not she continues to pursue us, that's up to her."

"I don't think it's that simple," replied Wander.

"Maybe not. But maybe it is. Maybe it would be better for her if it were," said Awen. "It does change things, though."

"Change things?" said Rucksack. "How so?"

"The moment we left the char, left Galway Ruin, left the Black Road, she found us. Odds are she's been tracking us for a while, presumably since Shantermon. But only now could she find us." Awen shook her head. "There were ways I was hoping we could go, and eventually leave this road and take different paths. Our way leads to England, and I had hoped to take a ferry across the Irish Sea. Those ways are closed to us now."

"Are you saying that the only way forward is for us to stay on the Black Road?" said Rucksack.

"As long as we travel we can't leave the road again," said Awen. "Not so much for food and water. The going only gets tougher from here. But we will go quickly, and hopefully we can put enough distance between us and this hound of souls that she cannot catch up to us again. "We just have to make it to the coast, south of Dublin. But when we get to the coast..." Awen's face got grimmer and grimmer. "Well, you'll just have to see for yourselves."

26

LUCKY

Across Ireland, the trio moved. The Black Road slowed them down, but fear quickened their pace to compensate.

"We might be getting near Dublin, but sooner or later she's going to catch up to us," said Rucksack as they laid out their blankets on the Black Road. A darker absence of light told them that night had come, and Awen had said they would grab a few hours' sleep before resuming their journey.

"We need to be fresh for the last stretch of Ireland," replied Awen. "We've made good time these last couple of days, but we have to rest awhile. We'll take turns keeping watch. I'll go first."

"She won't come for us here," said Wander.

"You can't know that," said Rucksack.

"No, you can't know that," Wander snapped back. "You weren't in her mind. It was like it was when you were reliving The Blast, only more... intimate. Closer. I could feel her life, her memories, her feelings, as if she and I were the same." Wander grimaced and shuddered.

"It was that bad," said Rucksack, his voice gentler.

Wander nodded. "She followed us to the village—that's where the guru told her to go, because as far as he knew, we would still be there, captured, waiting. She thought this was going to be simple."

"She is obedient, and that makes her driven," said Awen. "She won't stop pursuing, and she will take whatever advantage she can. But that obedience... there's a pride in her too. Makes her over-confident."

Rucksack gave a small grin. "We can use that."

"That's just it," said Wander. "She did think she would find us, take me, and go back to this guru in glory. Now she's having to move fast, think on her feet. I don't get the impression she's as accustomed to that. From what I could see, Róisín and the villagers nearly had her, but Fiach barely got away. She came to the Black Road, knowing that's what we were following, but she can't walk on it. It... I think it dulls her senses. She can't sense me, and it's even harder for her to travel it than it is for us. For us it's annoying and a little debilitating, but for her it's brutal. Every step is agony. I don't know why. Whatever it is about her that has such a keen sense of what makes someone like me different, maybe the Black Road, all that death, all those lives lost, maybe it overwhelms her. That's the best I can figure. Either way, she won't be following us."

"She'll follow the road in parallel," said Wander. "That's why we have to stay ahead of her, so she doesn't have a chance to ambush us farther along."

Later, Wander woke from a deep sleep. Sleep, oddly enough, had been easier here. There were things Wander had made peace with, just before falling into this world. Back home, sleep had been a challenge, but here Wander felt a greater peace than ever. They slept on death and ash, a mile-wide bedroll of burned bones. The dimness that hovered over the road hid the stars and the moon. Yet ever since arriving, Wander had slept deeply, soundly, and woke with a sense of fulfillment that hadn't been present since before the tornado took everything.

Wander went over to Awen, who nodded. "Ah, I didn't even

need to wake you," said Awen. "All these years, and I'm ready for a kip. Shame of it is, I don't sleep as well lately. That damn shadow is always hanging over my dreams." Awen stopped talking there, but Wander sensed that the shadow also hung over something else, something that Awen didn't want to talk about.

"I'll watch as long as I can," said Wander. "You and Rucksack get what rest you can."

"You have a kindness in you," replied Awen. "A goodness. You have a hard skin, and that makes sense, given what's happened to you and the life you've lived. The road toughens you. It can bring out all the light in the world, but the traveler is a person of solitude. There's a darkness in that solitude that we cannot run from, no matter where in the world we go. I often think the key to all this is just keeping the two in balance, that light and that dark."

"Is that advice for me?" Wander asked. "It seemed like this must be the part of the journey where I have a heart-to-heart with our group's fearless leader."

"It's advice that has always served me well," replied Awen. "But it didn't come from me."

"From who, then?"

Awen nodded toward Rucksack, who was sound asleep.

"It's still hard to believe that he's what you say he is," said Wander. "But I've seen it in him now. The goodness. The strength."

"He will always protect you," said Awen. "Just as he will always protect the world. It's who he is. Those he cares about, he will tend to them beyond all ruin. Including his own."

"I'm a job," replied Wander. "A means to an end. You needed a way to get him motivated, because he was so disjointed and dispirited after waking up."

"I won't deny that you made a handy catalyst to get him going again, to make him want to find a way for himself, by way of helping you find your way in a new world." Awen grinned. "Part of being the light of the world is knowing your own darkness."

"Or you're just a deviant old woman."

Awen chuckled. "Well said. I'm not above the deviance of age. I rather think it keeps me spry."

Wander couldn't help but laugh too. With Awen there was an ease, a constant brightness that Wander took great comfort in. "I'm lucky," said Wander. "Something so strange happens to me. Yet in all this big world, I meet up with the people who can help me, and are willing to do so."

"We make our own luck, Wander of the road," said Awen. "Sounds to me like it was simply time for yours to get cashed in."

"In case the chance doesn't come again," said Wander. "I want to thank you for helping me."

"You're welcome," said Awen. "But you are helping too."

"I can't hold my own in a fight the way you and Rucksack can."

"You don't have to. You have a sense to you, Wander," said Awen. "An understanding of the heart. You might not be from this world, but you seem to grasp it pretty well."

"Maybe our worlds aren't so different after all," said Wander.

"Or maybe you just have enough fresh perspective to see things and people here as they really are." Awen grinned. "Well, mostly."

"What's that supposed to mean?"

"The thing about having a late-night chat with a wandering sage," said Awen, "is that you never get the whole answer. Part of the story is left unfinished, because part of your role in the story is to live its completion."

"You are vague and frustrating too. I also want to mention that in case I don't get another chance."

"And you are headstrong and foolish, and you doubt yourself too much," said Awen. She grinned and tilted her head toward Wander. "As long as we're being open and honest while we can. Trust this world. Trust yourself. Trust those around you. Above all, trust your heart. You'll see clearly when you need to, and you'll do what you need to do."

Wander sat back. "Funny. That's not the first time I've been told that. Someone... Someone helped me understand what happened to me. With the tornado and my family. As if it had a message for me. And what you said... that's what, in the end, the tornado was telling me. Only apparently it was pretty important, given the price."

"That is a burden you will always carry," said Awen. "But living the truth of what you know will make that burden easier."

"Awen?" said Wander.

"Yes?"

"Do you love Rucksack?"

"Dearly," said Awen. "He is the brother I never had, and in many ways he is the son I never had. He is the dearest friend I have ever known. When someone helps you find your truest self, you hold them in a regard above all others. I met him at his lowest and worst, but even then, I could see the best in him." Awen leaned forward and kissed Wander on the forehead. "And in you, my child, brought here unknowingly, against your will, I have seen the best in you too. You don't yet see it. But in time you will."

With that, Awen rose and went over near Rucksack, then lay down and went to sleep.

While keeping watch, Wander took the painting from the daypack and stared at the strange scene: the person at the precipice, the hand reaching. Then Wander put it away, and waited—if not for the sun to rise, then for the darkness to fade, and in the absence of light to find a way.

27

———

THE IMPOSSIBLE ROAD

"Oh yes you damn well are."

The words alone were loud enough to wake Wander, but it was the heat in Awen's voice that had Wander up and running.

"I've told you I'm not," replied Rucksack.

Awen held out the scabbarded swords again. "Not ready. Not brave enough. Not sure. You know what I'm not, old friend? I'm not giving a damn."

"I can't wield them."

"Fine," said Awen. "Then I suppose no one will." She dropped the swords on the ash. A gray and black cloud puffed into the air as she walked away from Rucksack and the swords.

"Awen?" Rucksack ran after her.

"No." Awen slammed the end of her staff into the char. "You don't want to wear them? They're not mine to keep anymore. I prefer my staff anyway."

"I can't be trusted—"

"You can be trusted just as much as you always were, you feckin eejit," said Awen. "The one who saved the world, who saved all life, the one who Wander is relying on. You can be trusted with all these things. Yet you're afraid to slap some bits of wood and metal on your back."

"The Blast, Awen. It's all my fault—"

Awen socked him in the nose. He staggered back but did nothing else, only covered his face with his hands. Awen's voice was low, even rumbling, like thunder or the growl of a circling tiger. "You came to me burned, bleeding, and broken," she said. "A terrible burden on your back. You told me your story, and you made it clear that all the blame lay solidly on you. My previous life died in The Blast, and my future burned too. I had every right to kill you. Yet instead of killing you, or instead of turning you over to the plenty of people who would have gladly killed you, I forgave you. I tended your wounds. Hid you, gave you a place to rest and to lay down your burden. For a hundred years I watched you. Saw that you were alive and healing. Tell me, my friend, have I asked anything in return?"

"Awen," said Rucksack, "o' the love I bear you, I would have done the same."

"Well that's just feckin peachy," said Awen. "I love you too, my friend, but as our friend from another world would say, I am cashing in." She came over to Rucksack and stood right in front of him, her nose almost touching his. "You owe me, Faddah Rucksack. Here's my price: All the love and trust and forgiveness that I gave you, you now must give yourself."

"But I—"

"If you won't, then you might as well have let yourself die in that cave. You're here. Alive and able. You want redemption? You want a chance, and you want to make sure this world keeps having chances? Then stop nancying about with all this guilt and bollocks. Help Wander. Be the hero you have inspired others to be and to want to be. And pick up those feckin swords."

Awen turned away. No one spoke. Rucksack stared at the ground. Wander didn't move.

Then, with a sigh, Rucksack picked up the swords. He

strapped them onto his back. Awen gave him a curt nod but said nothing, only began to walk. Rucksack and Wander hurried to keep up.

By late morning they had passed by the southern outskirts of Dublin. Soon the air took on a salty tang: the refreshing, emboldening scent of the sea. Instead of walking through the middle of the Black Road, they decided they could chance walking closer to the northern edge. They could see the world beyond the Black Road, and that brought with it the bonus of a bit of light.

Beyond the edge of the road, grass gave way to sand that was white and light brown. The scent of ocean strengthened, and Wander drank in the lovely, vibrant scent of the sea.

They paused at the bottom of a dune. The blackened char blocked their view of the sea. Beyond it was the coast, and the Irish Sea, and across from there, England. "I'm going to warn you," said Awen. "This next part... is a bit shocking. Even given what we've seen so far."

"What could possibly be more shocking?" said Rucksack.

"You'll see," said Awen. "Just remember, The Blast burned its way across Ireland to England, from island to island."

With that, Awen walked briskly up the dune. The others sped up to stay near her.

At the top of the dune, they stopped again. And Wander gasped.

The Black Road ran down the dune and across a wide expanse of beach, easily half a mile from the bottom of the dune to the lapping waves. The dark scar of the char cut through the beach.

And into the sea.

"How..." said Rucksack, struggling to find the words. "How is this possible?"

"It shouldn't be," said Awen. "And for that it's called the impossible road."

The Black Road didn't just cut across the sand.

It cut through the sea.

"From what anyone can tell, The Blast cut down into the water, boiling away the sea where it touched," said Awen. "And the force kept going, into the sand and rock beneath the waves. It must have been a terrifying sight. Molten rock blasting upward like an erupting volcano, all the way across the sea. What you see goes from here all the way to the coast of England on the other side. The Blast bored down into the rock, but as the molten rock kept spraying upward, eventually it cooled and hardened on either side. And then it began to build on itself. The Blast not only parted the sea, it kept the way open."

Before them, on both edges of the mile-wide Black Road, dark rock rose in a wall, fifty feet thick, that prevented the sea from filling in the old wound and healing itself.

Between the rock walls, between the waves, the Black Road continued.

"It follows the natural slope of the seabed," said Awen. "At the bottom it levels out, and then you'll walk on the bottom of the sea. Over the years, it came to be called Bóthar Idir Tonnta, the Road Between Waves."

"You're saying that we're going to cross the Irish Sea," said Wander, "but go underneath it?"

"No," said Awen. "Between it."

"Wait a minute." Rucksack stared at their guide. "What do you mean *'you'll* walk?'"

"We are at the edge of Ireland," said Awen. "I have guided you as best I can, helped you find a way. But it has only been my job to get you going. I can go no farther. You now must continue on yourselves."

"You can't," said Wander. "We need you."

"If this is because o' earlier," said Rucksack, "you were right. I'm sorry. I wallowed in self-pity. I see right now."

"That's not it. You both are experts at finding your own way," replied Awen. "If I continue, I will only hinder you. Sooner or later, you'll come to over rely on my judgment, my leadership. A guide can lead only until the guided are ready to lead themselves. You're ready."

"We can't do this without you," said Rucksack. "I'm ready to take up the swords—"

"You have no choice but to be ready," said Awen. "You know it as well as I do. If you're going to find a new path, you can't do it with me leading the way. You have to lead yourself. You'll make mistakes. You'll have problems. But even if neither of you trust yourselves enough, I trust you both."

"Awen," said Wander. "Please."

But Awen shook her head, and she set the end of her staff firmly on the char of the Black Road. "You have a long road to go, my friends." Her voice was heavy and thick. "I will miss you. I hope that we may yet someday find each other again, even if only in dreams and memories."

Awen hugged each of them, and kissed each of them on the forehead. "Go with all my love," she said. "Go with the light of Ireland, of the world—and of yourselves. Stay true to each other, and you will always find your way."

Rucksack stared at her. "Awen..."

"Please, Rucksack. It's time. You know it. You came back. Now you must go forward."

His eyes widened. "No, Awen—it's her. Watch out!"

Fiach leaped onto the Black Road, just behind Awen. Awen turned. Fiach swung a long knife toward Awen, but the discomfort of the Black Road threw off her aim. Awen jumped backward and thrust out her staff at Fiach, knocking her away from the edge, deeper onto the Black Road.

They fought, staff and knife swinging, missing, connecting.

Rucksack reached back toward his swords.

"No!" yelled Awen. "Rucksack, no! Take Wander and go. It's the only way now. I will do all I can, but you have to go. Get as far away as you can. Go, you damn fool, go!"

"Awen!" yelled Wander. But Rucksack grabbed Wander by the arm, and they turned and ran.

Wander couldn't see Awen now. Wander and Rucksack ran to the shoreline, down the char, past the end of the long black wall. They descended the slope of the sea floor, on the path of the Bóthar Idir Tonnta. The sounds of screams and clangs followed them between the waves—then there was a scream, a crack like a staff snapping in two, a growl like a dog's, and then nothing but a horrible silence.

PART III

28

BETWEEN THE WAVES

"We never should have left her."

Rucksack sighed. The argument had been going all day, as constant as the sound of waves crashing on the rock a hundred feet above their heads as they made their way along the Bóthar Idir Tonnta.

"Maybe we should have feckin left you," said Rucksack. He walked faster, moving away from Wander.

"Prick."

"Prat."

Staring at Rucksack's back, Wander tried to think of where the argument had begun. The sounds of Awen and Fiach fighting had hardly stopped ringing in their ears when the waves became everything they heard. That and the sniping.

Three times Wander had tried to turn back. Three times Rucksack had turned them forward again.

They had walked for hours. By now Awen's body was likely cold on the beach. Or she was hurt, and hoping without hope that her friends would return.

More importantly, though, Rucksack's back was turned.

Wander spun on a heel and started back toward Ireland.

Moments later, Rucksack stood between Wander and whatever had happened to Awen. This time, though, he didn't speak, didn't grab Wander by the arm, nothing. He drew a scabbarded sword and stared hard at Wander.

"I promised to help you in whatever way I can," he said. "If you want to explore this world and find a place in it, I'll help you. Feck, if you could go back to your world and I could get you home, I would get you there. But no one said you had to walk. Awen said to help you, and that's what I will do."

"Friends don't abandon each other," said Wander. "We have to go back for her."

"You care so much about Awen? She did everything she could to give us a head start," said Rucksack. "It's a damn fool way to repay all her kindness, to keep trying to go back so you can play right into the hands of this damn guru."

"She needs our help."

"She needs us to trust her," replied Rucksack. "She told us to get moving. That's what we're going to do."

Wander started walking back toward Ireland again. Rucksack raised the sword back and above his head. His hand shook a little, but there was no fear in Rucksack's eyes. Only anger, and something else, but Wander couldn't figure out what it was.

"You wouldn't hit me," said Wander.

His mouth was flat and sharp. "I can knock you out without leaving a mark. It'll barely hurt."

"Oh, you're going to carry me to England, are you?"

Rucksack shrugged. The sword still trembled, but neither it nor Rucksack's gaze wavered. "After The Blast," he said, his voice low and broken, "I was burned and hurt. Badly. Thought I was going to die."

"But you didn't," Wander replied. "You fell asleep, sure, and you healed. Now you're here. Being a right pain in the arse."

"I didn't just walk to Clifden," he said. "I could barely stand. I figured I might as well just lie down and die. But I didn't." He leaned forward. "Do you know why?"

Wander shrugged.

"My mother was gone," he said, "lost in the fires. But I found my father's body. Hurt though I was, I couldn't let him just stay there."

"No. You didn't... You couldn't." The blood drained from Wander's face.

Rucksack nodded. "I carried my father's body from Galway to Clifden. A hundred miles, over the ash, over the hills, through the peat bogs, night and day. It took three days. I didn't stop walking. Sheer momentum was the only thing that kept me upright. If I stopped, I knew I wouldn't start again."

Wander thought of after the tornado. Everything and everyone gone. Being set down in a field, far away from everything Wander had ever known, far away from the name that might as well have been destroyed in the tornado too.

Rucksack took a step toward Wander. "When I showed up at Awen's doorstep, I told her everything. She didn't know me. And here I was, telling her that I was responsible for what had happened. She could have turned me away. Feck, I know what and who she had lost in The Blast. She'd have had every right to kill me. But she didn't. She took me in. Trusted me. Forgave me. And she helped me. Still is helping me, after a hundred years. I know when she's right—as you saw when I wouldn't take my swords back up."

"People like Awen never know when they're the ones who need saving," said Wander. "This is for her good. For all the ways she's helped us. We owe her that."

"She doesn't need saving," said Rucksack. "She needs us to do what she said. She's earned it. So either you damn well accept that we're moving on, or I'm going to lay you out."

Fury fumed inside, but Wander said nothing. He was so impossible. So frustrating. So—

Wander turned back toward England, away from Awen, and began to walk again. Rucksack returned the sword to his back and followed. Neither spoke. Their silence seemed less an absence of words and more a drowning of the fiery anger of all the things they weren't saying aloud but were screaming inside.

"I thought we were becoming friends," said Wander at last.

Rucksack didn't look back. "So did I."

Wander's eyes felt hot, but nothing around them was so much as warm. The sea floor was cool and refreshing, yet clammy and cold. The rock sucked away all the heat, and the sunlight barely came down to the bottom of the sea. They walked in a dim half-light, shadows melting into the rock wall until it was hard to tell where the sea floor ended and the rock wall began.

Wander followed the rock wall again, from the bottom of the sea to the top of the waves. The sea was out there, separating Ireland from England, and now separated from itself by The Blast. The sea never stopped bashing the rocks above. How strong were those rocks? Sure, they'd held for a century, but no spell was holding them in place, no magic but physics and inertia. The rocks could give way at any moment. Whenever rock stood against water, water always won—it was just a matter of when.

Now and then an especially large wave would strike, and sea spray would mist down. On the one hand the mist was refreshing, bracing. But every time it happened, Wander's heart raced, getting in all the beats it could before the waves would come crashing down, and the rocks would come crashing down, and all too soon both would stop Wander's heart. What an awful way to die: crushed under rocks at the bottom of the reclaiming sea.

Wander stared upward again, at the shadowy gash the rock made in the gray sky. So far, so good.

"What the feck?" Rucksack stopped walking, and Wander almost crashed into him.

"What?"

"Look forward instead of away," replied Rucksack with

wonder in his voice.

Before them rose a massive wall built of the same black rock and as high as the walls holding back the waves. The wall blocked the road—but a wide passage, barred by a gate, had been cut through it.

Wander's mouth fell open. "No freakin way."

"Ten thousand years," said Rucksack, "and I've never seen anything like this."

"I guess Awen didn't get a chance to mention it."

"No," said Rucksack. "But she trusted us. To find in ourselves the strength, guidance, and understanding to do what needed to be done." He sighed. "She's right. It's the only way. Otherwise we would become too dependent on her leadership. Look at us, Wander. Bickering like children."

Wander nodded. "We should be helping each other. Right now, we're all we've got."

Looking at him anew, Wander could see a softness in the dark eyes that hadn't been there before. A vulnerability showed itself, behind all the glory and the guilt, the strength and the fear.

Together they looked ahead again, still amazed at the sheer impossibility of the wall, the road, and the gate. The Blast had not created these things. These things had been built.

Wander couldn't help but smile. "So much has happened. I've been forgetting to appreciate all this," said the traveler. "I'm in a different world. A world that is both familiar and brand new. I'm forgetting that I'm a wanderer. I should be taking in all of this. I should be blown away."

Rucksack grinned too. "So you're ready?"

"Of course. We're on an impossible road, walking between the waves across the bottom of the sea between two countries. You bet your arse I'm ready to find out how in the hell this could be here too."

They began moving forward again. As they approached, the gate opened.

29

GATE

"Who are you and what is your business here?" asked the guard inside the gate. He had opened the outer gate to let them into a small chamber where he waited. Behind him, a sheer wall of black rock rose nearly to the full height of the chasm, blocking their view of what lay beyond. Set in the black wall behind him, another gate remained closed and locked.

"Business where?" said Wander. "What is this place?"

"This is Dodhéanta, the impossible city," said the guard. "The city between the waves."

The two travelers looked at each other, then Rucksack turned to face the guard again. "We are Rucksack and Wander," said Rucksack. "We have business in England, but we couldn't make the crossing via ship."

"All visitors must have something to offer," said the guard. "What do you have to offer?"

"We offer such aid as the city may need," replied Rucksack.

Wander had a feeling the city must need aid aplenty. Armed only with a long staff, the guard wore a gray sort of jumpsuit adorned with no finery, no fancy helmet or crazy bits and bobs. Everything about him seemed dingy and careworn, especially his gray face, dull eyes, and flat voice. There was a dampness to him that Wander figured must be due to living where sea spray is constantly falling on you. The guard kept glancing back toward the inner wall, as if either he was afraid to be outside of the gates, or he dreaded having to return.

Wander looked up to the top of the cliffs again.

"What's wrong?" said Rucksack.

"This place creeps me out," said Wander. "It's like a fear of heights in reverse. Fear of depths."

"Perhaps," said the guard, "you do not wish to be here after all."

"No," said Rucksack. "We do. We just... We did not know this was here. Our guide who helped us to the shore of Ireland did not have a chance to tell us."

"You had not heard of the city?" said the guard.

"We... We are from a long way away," replied Wander.

The guard looked from one to the other, as if staring at the tension between them. Then he shook his head. "I'm sorry," said the guard. "This city is a place of peace. Whatever you bring with you, whatever discord lies between you, we cannot have it here."

Wander stared at him, surprised at the guard's eloquence.

"But we have to be able to pass through here," said Wander. "We are being pursued. Someone wants to hurt us. They are following us, and we don't know how much time we have before they catch up."

"I feel for your plight," said the guard. "I wish you well. But you may not enter."

"We can't turn back!" said Wander.

The guard shrugged. "You don't have to," he replied. "You can always climb up."

Wander paled. The guard ushered them back through the outer gate, then closed and locked it.

30

GUARDED

"Please," said Rucksack again. "We are on a matter of urgency. My..." He cleared his throat and would not look at Wander. "My companion... Someone is pursuing us... Please."

The guard said nothing, and did not even look at them. He went over to a little bench in the little area between the outer and inner gates. He sat down and stared, saying nothing. He only looked beyond the gate, always on watch for whoever might approach on the road between the waves.

Rucksack shook his head. "If Awen were here we'd already be inside."

Wander stared at him, eyes widening. "You're right." Wander smacked the bars of the gate. "Hey, guardy guy."

The guard looked outward, ignoring Wander and saying nothing.

"We have to go this way," said Wander. "We were told this is the road we had to take, and if your city is on the road, then we were meant to come through here. You have to let us in. Please. The Awen of Ireland sent us."

The guard's eyes flicked to Wander, but still he said nothing.

"Awen traveled with us until the coast, but we were attacked and Awen fought the attacker to buy us time. We... We fear Awen is dead," said Wander. "Her last instruction was for us to follow the road between the waves. If you know who she is, if she matters at all to this place, then you have to let us in."

Wander stared at the guard, waiting, hoping. Without a word, the guard stood and walked away.

Tense minutes slowly passed.

Then the guard came back—but not alone.

The woman was dressed in green and white, the dress simple but elegant. She was older, perhaps the same age as Awen looked. Her long hair flowed down in silver and white.

"I am Emmanua," she said, "leader of Dodhéanta, the city between the waves. I have been told that the Awen of Ireland sent you, and that you are Rucksack and Wander."

They nodded and went to the gate, all the while avoiding looking at each other.

"We know the Awen of Ireland," said Emmanua. "In many a trying time in the founding, building, and maintaining of Dodhéanta, she has been our friend. I had thought she would be with you. There is much I would discuss with her."

"We are being pursued by a most dangerous person," said Rucksack, "who set upon us at the entrance to the road to your city."

"Awen sacrificed her safety to buy us time," said Wander. "We don't know what happened to her, though. We know only that she sent us down this road—and she knew the road led here."

Emmanua's face was grave. "Awen sent word of your coming, and I was hopeful. That she is not here saddens me greatly. Yet you were in her care, and she said that she hoped we could offer aid and shelter for your time here. All of which I would happily provide."

Emmanua looked from one of them to the other. "Yet I am told that you come here in some discord. This is a city of peace. We live in close quarters, as you can imagine, and we live always in the shadow and threat of the sea and the rock. We cannot allow undue conflict here."

"Please," said Wander. "If Awen—"

"I am not finished," said Emmanua. "Your saving grace is the word of the Awen herself vouching for you. She told me only that you each are seeking something. I want to honor my friend, especially if her dedication to you is such that she was willing to risk her life for you. Yet you can imagine the argument within myself. I must protect my city and those who live here, even at the risk of offending a friend. If you are to enter, can you set aside your differences while you are here?"

They agreed. Wander started to say something else, but a shake of Rucksack's head made Wander stop.

"I am willing to allow you inside," said Emmanua. "But I have a condition."

Rucksack took a step forward. "Name it."

"You say that now," said Emmanua, "but you are desperate and don't know what I'll ask of you. I'm just as aware of that as you are." At a nod from Emmanua, the guard opened the outer gate.

"I imagine the problem is dire and threatens all here," said Rucksack.

"Whatever it is, we will help," said Wander. "We will make it right. Terrible or noble, we will meet your price."

The guard closed the outer gate behind them, then unlocked the inner gate. As it opened, Wander smiled at Rucksack. He smiled back.

Emmanua led Rucksack and Wander through the gate, beyond the rock wall that had blocked their view of the impossible city beyond. Then, with a start and a gasp, Wander stopped.

31

THE WATER

Before them lay a high sea of green. Buildings rose, deep green with white veins, angular yet well crafted, up to five stories high, and they filled the mile-wide space between the black walls. People moved down straight roads, not black but the same green as the buildings, designed to make the compact space feel airier and bigger than it was. Despite the dimness, Wander saw flower boxes and small gardens in the fronts of what were clearly homes and other buildings.

The people did not have the guard's dourness. Conversation flowed everywhere. Children skipped down the streets, laughter bubbling behind them. People's clothes were simple but finely made, and the buildings had small etchings and carvings, details made with vision and care.

"How... How could this be?" said Wander.

Emmanua chuckled. "You were expecting to see a bunch of grumpy taciturn survivors, barely clinging to life?"

"That wasn't exactly what was going through my mind," replied Wander.

Emmanua laughed. "It's not the first time I've seen that look on the face of a new visitor," she said. "The guards are well trained to look worn and dour. It still amazes me how often that alone can make people turn back. What they never learn is that we live simply but well, and with much happiness."

"But... how?" said Rucksack. "How do you have food and fresh water here? How have you made this place?"

"For many years after The Blast," said Emmanua, "none would travel the Black Road. The world feared it, and understandably so. Yet one day, my mother found herself caught between an existence with no true life, and a road where no one else would go."

"Why?" asked Wander. The desperation made sense—it was why they were there too—but what could have forced a young woman to travel this perilous path?

"Because of me," said Emmanua. "She was pregnant, but out of wedlock. She had been shunned by family and friends in Dublin, and all but forced out of the city—not that life there had been all that grand anyway. She was abandoned by all she had known. Leaving south, she came to the Black Road, and she did not know what do. Then, from out of the west, someone approached. Someone who was doing what she had never heard of anyone doing. This person was walking the Black Road." Emmanua smiled. "Can you guess who that person was?"

Rucksack chuckled, though Wander could hear the pain in his voice.

Emmanua nodded and continued. "Awen found my mother, and my mother decided to walk with this curious woman. Along the way they spoke of many things, and walked together to the sea, to the black rock where the road continued between the waves. She and Awen said farewell. At first my mother considered walking to England and starting over. Along the way, though, she found the most curious thing."

Their own wandering had taken them through the city, and at every turn Wander was amazed. Despite the dimness, the green buildings had a luminous softness, as if a light shone inside the stone, giving the city a soft glow.

As they passed a ring of two-story buildings, the way opened into a large open circular space that was green and full of people chatting and children playing. At the center of the plaza, a fountain bubbled.

"This is what my mother found," said Emmanua, running her fingers through the water. "A little stream. She was thirsty, then she heard the gurgling. She stopped here and ran her hands through the water. Then she wondered something." Emmanua put her cupped hand into the stream, then raised her hand to her lips. "Do you wonder the same thing?"

Rucksack and Wander filled their hands as well. Wander's hand tingled at the water's chill. Waiting for the sharp brininess of the salty sea surrounding them, Wander drank.

Eyes wide, Wander stared at Emmanua. "There's no salt," said Wander. "This is fresh water."

Emmanua nodded. "Exactly. A spring of fresh water, at the bottom of the sea. Pure as light. The moment my mother drank it, she understood: Where water flows, people live." They each took another drink. "Mother decided that instead of going to England, she would stay here. Her home, her city, had rejected her, and she had no guarantee of a warm welcome across the sea. So she decided she would make her own home, her own city, here, in this impossible place." Emmanua raised her arms and turned in a slow circle, the older woman for a moment like a dancing young girl.

"For years she went back and forth," said Emmanua. "She had no money, nothing but the clothes on her back. She returned to Ireland and spoke to many people about what she planned to do. Most thought she was mad, of course. An unmarried woman with a baby, trying to build a city in the middle of the sea, while Ireland was struggling to rebuild after The Blast. Others listened to her, though—people who also had no true place of their own, but they had means, trades, resources. Together they figured out how to live here, and grow the simple edible plants that sustain us. They figured out how to channel the fresh water, track its flow for tapping in other parts of the city. We figured out services we could offer other parts of the world, and from there grew a small but useful economy."

"And the rock?" said Wander.

Rucksack grinned. "Connemara marble," he said.

"Yes," said Emmanua. "Awen helped make that happen."

"Has she come here?" asked Rucksack.

"Many times over the years, though it taxed her greatly to step foot off Ireland. Awen was one of my mother's closest advisors and friends. Awen was midwife when I was born. She was here when I was named, and sometimes visited while I was growing up. She wasn't around much, but she always had a way of being here when she was needed." Emmanua's face darkened. "Except now. Come. You will be my personal guests. Once you are settled in, I will tell you of the task you face."

They continued their journey. On the far side of the plaza, they went to a simple building that looked no different than the others. "This is my home," said Emmanua. "The fountain is the heart of the city, but this is the mind. This is where we determine the course of the city, how we grow and change, who may live here, how we conduct trade."

"Yet you always keep in sight o' your heart," said Rucksack.

"Exactly. This city exists because we live together, work together, and trust in the best of each other. We have our differences, but so far we have found ways to resolve them peacefully."

Inside the simple home, Emmanua showed Rucksack and Wander to their rooms. The three went their separate ways.

Day faded into evening, and the three reconvened in a small but spacious sitting room that took up the entire space of the second floor. There was a desk and some simple yet comfortable chairs. Open windows let them look out in all directions, from the fountain in the plaza to the edge of the city to the neighboring buildings on either side.

Near windows overlooking the plaza and its bubbling foun-tain, they sat at a simple but well-crafted marble table, and a meal was brought. "I will now explain your task," said Emmanua. She raised her green goblet. "Please drink with me."

Rucksack and Wander raised their goblets too.

Then spat seawater across the table.

"What is this?" said Rucksack.

"My explanation," replied Emmanua. "The water in these goblets is from my own kitchen."

Salt stung Wander's mouth. "You said the underground spring was tapped, so everyone in the city drinks fresh water."

"That's the problem," said Emmanua. "All over the city, the water is going from fresh to salty. We've tried to figure out why, but so far have been unable to. Some have even gone up the wall, to seek a solution there."

"What did they find?"

Emmanua's face paled, and for a moment she looked away. "They did not return."

32

CLIMB

The next morning, watery sunlight drifting down into the city, Rucksack and Wander stood at the bottom of the black rock wall.

"I don't know if I can do this." Wander looked up. And up. And up. Over a hundred feet the wall rose.

"We can find those people who have gone missing," said Rucksack. "Maybe they're hurt. Maybe there's some threat up there that Emmanua didn't know about."

"And if we don't, we get kicked out of the city and probably run into Fiach on the way back." Wander stared at the wall some more, certain it had gotten even taller. "It's a lie, but maybe I could do with being told this isn't complete lunacy."

Rucksack smiled. "This isn't complete lunacy."

Wander tried to chuckle, but couldn't. The top of the wall was as far away as the sun. Wander's breath kept catching, and everything felt cold and clammy. "Maybe this isn't the right way after all," said Wander. "Awen isn't perfect. She could have been wrong about this. About me. About going this way. Maybe we should just leave. Turn back toward Ireland. Fiach won't see that coming. She's probably been turned away already and is on her way back.

We could get the jump on her, Rucksack. That sounds brilliant. Then keep going. You and I get back to Ireland... and we see what happens."

"So eager to be rid o' me that you'd face Fiach and whatever this guru has in store for you," Rucksack replied. "Feckin charmed I am."

Tears stung Wander's eyes. "Heights terrify me. The thought of climbing up this sheer rock scares me so much I'm surprised I don't just fall dead on the spot."

Rucksack reached for Wander's hand, but Wander stepped away. "I'm not ungrateful," said Wander. "You've helped me. A stranger."

"A stranger," said Rucksack, shaking his head. "Was thinking we'd gotten beyond that. Then again, even at my age you still make plenty o' mistakes."

"Sorry," said Wander. "That's not what I meant."

"You're scared," said Rucksack. "I get it. But we have to see this through. I owe Awen more than you will ever know. And these people need help. If... If you had gone missing, I'd be looking for you."

Skin prickling, Wander looked away from Rucksack. The black rock was much easier to look at. "I know... but I don't think I can do this." The world spun, like it had those years ago, in the tornado, touching the sky and the clouds—

"Okay. Stay here." Keeping his gaze fixed on the wall, Rucksack started climbing. "I'll deal with this by myself. Wouldn't be the first time."

Wander took a step back, away from the wall, away from Rucksack. Then stopped. Wander stared at him. At the black rock wall and at how very, very high up it went. The world was liquid at the edges, nothing solid or clear anymore. But Rucksack kept climbing, and he was going up there alone.

"Dammit." Wander pushed away the memory of the tornado

and grabbed the rock. "No way I'm letting you deal with this yourself."

The moment Wander's feet left the ground, the world spun. Wander nearly let go—

"Breathe. Wander, breathe."

Wander looked up. Rucksack nodded, waiting. He almost smiled.

Wander breathed. The world came back into focus. Wander started climbing, and caught up to Rucksack. He nodded at Wander, then returned his gaze to the path up the rock above him. Wander was certain he had smiled.

"Ultimately you're here because of me," said Wander. "I can't let you do this alone. I won't be a coward and let you down."

"It's okay to be scared," said Rucksack. "Brave only happens when you're scared."

They kept climbing. Rucksack would occasionally look down, making sure that the fear wasn't getting the better of Wander.

"You sure you're okay?" he asked.

"Course I'm not okay," replied Wander through gritted teeth. "Every bit we go up, part of me wants to let go. Then I wouldn't have to be so afraid anymore."

"Wander," said Rucksack, "look at me."

"What?"

"You're going to get through this," he said. "You're strong. Stronger than you give yourself credit for. And much kinder too. But you care, and in that care is strength. The trick is to care more than you fear."

"Is it really that simple?"

"Yes," said Rucksack, and he grinned. "That and just look at the rock in front o' you."

Wander couldn't help but grin back, then they began climbing again.

They went higher. Wander ignored burning muscles and short

breath, slipping feet and raw fingertips. All that mattered was another hand higher, then another foot lifted up, then body, then other hand and other foot, and then all over again. All the while, Wander looked only at the rock. Rock that the fires of The Blast had scoured. Was black actually the rock's real color? If they were to drill into the seabed elsewhere, and find the rock beneath the eons of sand and settled decayed bits of former life, would the rock be black there too? Or would it be, say, green or gray or brown?

Pebbles scattered over Wander.

"Sorry," said Rucksack. "Slipped a little."

"Are you okay?"

"Let's just say I'll be glad when we're at the top."

The top. How far along were they? And Wander felt it, gaze shifting downward, away from the rock before Wander's eyes, wondering how far up they had come from the ground below.

Wander stopped just in time.

Instead of looking down, Wander paused, and breathed. The world was melting again, blurring and going indistinct. To look down might as well be to let go.

Wander's eyes closed.

"Wander, are you all right?"

At his voice, Wander's head lifted, and eyes opened—and there he was. Faddah Rucksack. The sun was stronger now, not as diluted, and there was an actual yellow warmth to the light. Rucksack hung on the wall, an outcropping of shadow, some weariness in his face, but mostly concern.

Just beyond him, the black rock ended at a squared edge. Beyond it Wander could see the blue of a calm bright sky.

"I'm all right," said Wander. "We're nearly there."

Still staring at the sky, Wander started to climb again. Not seeing Rucksack's face, Wander kept watching the sky, kept seeing the edge of the cliff become more distinct. Wander lifted a foot to go to another little ridge of stone.

Then slipped and began to fall.

Wander didn't turn, though. Didn't try to scramble to the rock. Just heard the air roaring by. Instead, Wander remembered that feeling of stepping through the shadow between the trees, that feeling of falling, terrifying, that last feeling before there wouldn't be any more feeling—

Yet there had been. Wander had come here.

But already the ground felt so close, too close. This fall would not have a new moment beyond. Just a sudden stop at the end.

Wander's eyes closed.

The roar was louder now. It filled what was left of Wander's world: darkness behind the closed eyes, the hope of sunlight nearly felt, and the roar, the roar—

Wander's fall stopped.

All breath flew away.

And then, with a gasp, came back.

Wander's eyes opened.

Rucksack's wide eyes burned as if he had brought the sun with him. Tension hung taut in his face as with one hand his fingertips gripped a small ledge of rock. His other arm was wrapped around Wander. Above the crashing of the waves, a sound like the roar of a tiger bounced off the rock wall.

With a shout, Rucksack swung them back toward the face of the rock, and Wander grabbed onto it again. They climbed. After countless lifts and steps and breaths, Wander reached up and touched not rock, but air. Then a gloved hand locked around Wander's wrist.

Wander climbed off the wall and onto the top.

"Well done," said Rucksack.

"At least we survived," replied Wander, looking out over the rocky expanse. Waves crashed over the far edge, but no water reached across the otherwise dry stone. "Now let's find those people."

33

MOMENT OF TRUTH

"I don't know what to do," said Wander.

"Spoken like a true hero," replied Rucksack. "Truth is, we rarely have a plan. It happens even less often that we have any feckin clue whatsoever what we're going to do in any given situation."

"You've been winging it for ten thousand years?"

Rucksack shrugged. "So far so good. Though this problem is proving trickier than most."

"We've looked everywhere," said Wander. "But no sign of anything wrong. No missing people. We're missing something."

Frustration showed on Rucksack's face too. "I don't know what though. I've listened to the air and the water. I've touched the rock and asked it to tell us, but it's just a big damn bunch o' rock with the sea on one side and an impossible city on the other."

"We can't help these people if we can't find them," said Wander. They stood near each other, but not next to each other, facing in opposite directions. "How are we supposed to fix a problem when we can't find the source of it?"

"The odds are always against you," said Rucksack. "The stakes are always absurd—and higher than you first realized. There is never enough time, nor a perfect solution. There is only what you can manage at the time."

"Right now we can't manage anything though," said Wander. "Short of walking every bit of rock between Ireland and England, I don't see how we're going to find those people. Or maybe they're not here anymore. Maybe the ocean got them. Maybe someone took them."

"None o' this is right." Rucksack took a breath and sighed. They stared at the black, barren rock around them. "Moments like these have been my life," said Rucksack. "Every time the world has presented an impossible situation, I'm the one who's had to face the choice o' what to do. But this... I'm stumped."

Wander took Rucksack 's hand. "Me too," said Wander, "but at least they had someone looking for them."

"Surely there's someone who knows you're gone," said Rucksack.

Wander shrugged. "I had no one. Nobody is looking for me. No one will care that I'm gone. Maybe the guy who ran the hostel, but only because I needed to pay him."

Rucksack stared deep into Wander's eyes. "I'd look for you." His voice had softened and deepened, yet a tension fluttered through him like lightning.

The roar of the crashing sea faded. The two of them stood there, saying nothing. Just staring.

"It's making sense now," said Wander at last.

"Where the missing people are?" replied Rucksack.

"No, not that." Wander squeezed Rucksack's hand and took a step torward him. "This."

"What?"

"Ten thousand years old and you don't recognize it?" Wander chuckled. "Then again, I can't say much. I haven't had much practice either."

Rucksack tilted his head. "Practice at what?"

Wander kissed him.

When they let go, Rucksack stood there, eyes closed, a half-smile and a radiance on his face.

"You can open your eyes now," said Wander, leaving a kiss on Rucksack's cheek.

"I don't know what's wrong up here," said Rucksack, "but for me, it's as if we just fixed some fundamental part o' the universe."

Wander caressed Rucksack's face. "It'll do for now."

Then Rucksack looked away.

"What is it?"

They took hands and walked to the far edge of the wall. The Irish Sea crashed against the rocks.

Rucksack looked east. "You can just see England from here."

"That's encouraging," said Wander, "but what matters to me most right now is what I see right in front of me."

"And what's that?"

Wander touched his cheek. "Your face, you impossible, difficult, amazing, beautiful man. Just your face."

They kissed again, then returned to the other side of the wall. Below them, the green city went on.

"Rucksack," said Wander, "what are we going to tell Emmanua?"

"Granted I'm new to this," said Rucksack, "but isn't this sort o' thing private, you know, between two adults?"

Wander chuckled. "Not the part I meant."

"I know. And I don't know." Rucksack shook his head and looked around. "Nothing up here makes sense. Nothing seems wrong. Whatever happened to those people, there's no sign. Whatever's wrong, you can't tell from up here. I... I don't know what to do."

As if hidden in the crashing of the waves, Wander heard something. Shuffling, scraping sounds. Rucksack heard it too. They looked around but saw nothing.

Then they looked to the edge of the rock, where they had come up from the city.

A hand rose into the air and slapped the top.

34

THE PROBLEM

Green and white rustled in the sea breeze. Both feet firmly planted on the rocks at the top of the wall, Emmanua stood up. Weariness strained her face, and her hands had a slight tremble. But there was something else, something in her face that Wander kept coming back to. A question of sorrow and regret.

"Why are you here?" asked Wander.

"I had to check on you," replied Emmanua, "to see what has happened."

"The answer is not much," said Wander. "We've looked and looked. But we haven't found the missing people or figured out why the water is turning salty."

Emmanua nodded, sadness in her eyes. "And what of the two of you?" she asked. "You have been in such discord. I admit, I had many misgivings about you coming up here, but I hoped it would be for the best."

Rucksack stared hard at Emmanua. "We... We have figured out our differences, and why they were there." He took Wander's hand.

"*Were* there?" said Emmanua. Seeing their linked hands, she smiled. Some of the sadness left her face. "Now you see what I saw. That is something."

Wander took a step forward. "What you saw?" All the air and blood rushed from Wander. "You knew... how we felt?"

"Wander?" said Rucksack. "What is it?"

Dropping his hand, Wander stood in front of Emmanua, eyes blazing like Rucksack's. Wander spoke with a growl, like faraway thunder in a summer storm. "There's nothing wrong with the damn water, is there?"

"What are you talking about?" said Rucksack.

Emmanua said nothing, only stared at Wander.

"The salt water we had in your home, at your table," said Wander. "You said that the water had become salty. You lied."

"No," said Emmanua. "I said that the water had come from my kitchen. I let your minds fill in the rest. As you can imagine, we can easily access salt water too. Before I came to the gate to meet you, I filled a pitcher and brought it to my kitchen."

Wander took a step back. "We could have died."

Emmanua shrugged. "Sadly, all too often the threat of death is the only thing that makes us appreciate what matters most in life," she said. "Are you so confident you would have acknowledged your feelings in any other way?"

Wander started to reply, but stopped.

Rucksack stood next to Wander. "You deceived us."

Emmanua shrugged. "You were already deceiving yourselves. I could tell from the moment I first saw you. I understand. I too know what it is to resist love." The sadness returned to her eyes. "I have done many things that I am proud of. Dodhéanta is my family, my life's work. But even my brightest days have been tinged with the darkness of regret, for the one whose love I shared but refused to accept and return."

"When you told us the water was salty and those people were missing," said Rucksack, "you were trying to get us to see past our conflict. Have a common cause."

"It was the only way," said Emmanua. "Not just for your feelings. But for the hopes of your quest. Awen had written and told me everything. Seeing you at the gate, the tension and conflict there, I could tell that if you continued as you were, then you would fail. If you are to find your way, then first you have to know what you really are to one another."

"The water is safe," said Rucksack.

"As are we in the city," said Emmanua, with a small smile. "As safe as we ever are, anyway. None have come up here. None are missing. I hope you can forgive me."

"Forgive you?" said Wander. "I hate heights. I fell. I would have died if Rucksack hadn't caught me."

"I did not know about your fear," said Emmanua. "But I knew that come what may, as long as you were with Faddah Rucksack, you would come to no harm."

Wander's hands tightened into fists. "I don't know if I can say the same for you."

Rucksack laid a gentle arm in front of Wander. "Stop, Wander." He sighed. "She's right."

"She risked our lives."

"And in so doing, she saved our hearts."

Wander glared at Emmanua. "Dammit," said Wander. "But don't expect me to thank you."

"I hope that you will come down and be my guest," said Emmanua. "I would ask only that we may raise a glass together, and that you may be at peace while you are here."

"I could definitely do with a feckin drink after all this," said Wander. "As long as it's not salty."

They all went to the wall and began the long climb back down to the city.

35
_____

NIGHT

Wander took another pull from the pint of GPS, emptying the glass. Standing on top of the five-story building, the tallest in the impossible city, Wander could not hear the sea over the chatter and celebration in the plaza below. Every person in the city was there, greeting and chatting with the strangers who had wandered to their home between the waves. Even the guard who had first blocked their entry into Dodhéanta was there, laughing and joking and bringing fresh pints to Wander and Rucksack when they were both down below.

"You didn't want to hear again about how fascinated they are with your journey," said Rucksack. He came up from the staircase inside and handed Wander a fresh pint. They clinked glasses and drank deeply.

"No, I didn't," said Wander. "People talk about us almost like we're heroes. Maybe you are, but I'm not. I'm terrified. Of heights. Of Fiach. Of dying."

"O' us."

Wander said nothing.

"You care deeply, Wander o' the road, and I can tell that you fear most when you care most." Rucksack kissed Wander's cheek, his lips smooth and firm. "That's as it should be. That fear reminds you o' the depth o' your caring, and it reminds you to appreciate what you have with all you've got."

"I needed a break from the attention," said Wander. "We're guests. And novel ones at that. I get it. I just needed a breather."

Standing together, they stared out over the city. "It's peaceful up here," said Rucksack. "Though I must confess myself surprised."

"That of all the places I could have gotten some time to myself, I went up somewhere high?"

Rucksack nodded.

Wander grinned. "Maybe your bravery is rubbing off on me."

They kissed, touching each other's faces and embracing.

"This city is a fragile place," said Wander. "How long do you think they have?"

"Every place is fragile," replied Rucksack, "yet also strong and resilient. That's what makes these moments so special."

"We defy the odds against us," said Wander. "A bunch of life forms spitting in the face of impossible odds."

"Pretty much." Rucksack grinned. "It certainly keeps things interesting."

"Is that what has kept you going all this time?" asked Wander. "That thrill of defeating the odds?"

"Yes and no," said Rucksack. "It's a component."

"Life grinds people down."

Rucksack nodded. "Something our worlds have in common. In its own ways, life has ground down you and me. No one can escape it. But when we do something that helps, we renew what was lost. We restore some o' what life's toils and disappointments have ground away. That's what I live for."

"You want to restore that sparkle in people's eyes."

"Yes," said Rucksack. "I live for reminding them that amazing people can make amazing things happen in this amazing world."

"In my world they get called miracles."

"I'm familiar with the concept," said Rucksack. "Here we care more about people making their own miracles. World comes out a better place when people work at it instead o' expecting some all-powerful force to do everything for them."

"That's why Awen said there were stories of you, but no one really knows who you are." Wander stared at him. "You don't want to be known."

"The best heroes don't just save the day," said Rucksack. "They show others how to be their own hero. Then they get the feck out o' the way, fade out and let the world get on."

"I think I get that." Wander smiled. "You chose obscurity. You didn't want people to rely on you too much, so instead they would rely on themselves and those around them." Wander squeezed his hand and stared into his deep dark eyes. "You wanted people to know the deeds but not the doer. Then maybe they'd be more likely to realize that they could find in themselves the way to do great things too."

Rucksack stared back. "You and I, Wander... I think I understand why we had a hard time before."

Wander nodded. "We understand each other well enough that it can cut deep."

They kissed again.

"Ten thousand years," said Wander. "I can't be the first."

"Love?" Rucksack shrugged. "What if I said you were?"

Wander leaned back. "How could that possibly be?"

"Ever since I was a child, I've spent all my time saving the world, Wander. Dashing about all over the place, continent to continent. Always something to be doing. And my parents were still alive. We were a tight family. I cared only about them and what I had to do. Never had room in my life or heart for anyone else."

"So, no one ever caught your eye?" Wander grinned. "Or kissed you? Or..."

One corner of Rucksack's mouth turned upward. "No. Not till

you." He ran a hand through Wander's hair. "I had seen the attraction enough times, but never really felt it in myself. I'd felt that attraction from people, mind. But never felt it back."

Wander kissed him again.

"We can't stay here long." Rucksack's face darkened again. "Fiach is still out there. We have to keep moving."

Wander nodded. "And we will."

"We could sneak out o' the city tonight," said Rucksack. "Cover o' darkness and all that. Wouldn't take us long to get to England."

"We're safe tonight," said Wander.

"We are hunted."

Wander chuckled. "You're nervous. But it's going to be okay. I know what to do about Fiach."

"What are you going to do?"

"Something that can wait till morning." Wander took his pint and set both glasses down on the roof. They kissed, then Wander took Rucksack's hand and led him toward the stairs.

"Are we going back to the party?" asked Rucksack.

"Nope," said Wander. "We did something amazing today, and we are something amazing together. Tonight, we're done with the crowds and the celebrations and the recounting of deeds and journeys and all that stuff. You're right. We are hunted. We have no idea what tomorrow will be like, or what challenges we face next. We have no idea how long we have, or how all this will play out, for better or worse, for success or failure, for life or death. Anything can happen. But tonight we have safety. Tonight we have each other. We're not planning or running or fighting. For the moment we know we have, it is going to be just you and me. Alone. We have our own celebrating to do—and after ten thousand years, it's about time you got to."

36

THE REQUEST

In the late morning, after a few delays, a lavish breakfast, and a couple of breakfast pints, Emmanua and the entire city led Rucksack and Wander to the city's eastern gates.

"Are you ever going to tell me your plan?" Rucksack whispered as they walked.

Wander grinned. "Soon."

Emmanua came over and walked with them. "There is something you should know," she said. "Wander... you are not of this world."

"No, but it's not like I can go back, so it doesn't really matter."

Emmanua stared at Wander for a moment, as if weighing whether or not to continue. "What if I told you there was a way?"

"What?" said Rucksack.

"I know nothing of certainty. But go to London. Seek out Jade London there, at the Mirror & Phoenix, across from the Square of Ashes. She will be able to help you."

Wander and Rucksack nodded, but could find no words. Emmanua's voice bounced around Wander's mind. There might be a way home.

They stopped at the gates, which were still closed.

"Friends," said Emmanua. "You came to us in discord, but you have restored harmony." She grinned at the two of them, though Wander was certain there was a sly wink as well.

Emmanua continued. "You may count yourselves as honorary citizens of Dodhéanta. From now on, its gates will always open for you."

With that, the guards began to open the eastern gates. The green road of the city gave way to the Black Road. Beyond was more of the impossible road—but also, to the east, was England. They were over halfway across the Irish Sea now, yet as Wander glanced down the Black Road, there was an unexpected pang. A possibility of home.

Emmanua leaned over to Wander and began to speak in a low, measured tone. "As for what you asked me about," said Emmanua, "it's been seen to."

"We are grateful to you, Emmanua," said Wander.

"It's the least I can do to repay my deception," said Emmanua.

"I forgive you... though honestly, I thank you too. Now that I understand."

Emmanua rested a hand on Wander's shoulder and stared the traveler deep in the eyes. "Take care of each other. Go in whatever peace and love you can find in this difficult time."

Wander glanced from Emmanua to Rucksack and back. "I don't know anymore."

"Of course you don't," said Emmanua. "But I will tell you this: If it's meant to be, make it be. Just keep putting one foot in front of the other. You'll get where you are going. Then you can figure out for yourself if it's where you need to be."

"What about where I want to be?"

Emmanua shrugged. "One of the greatest things in life is when what we want and what we need are one and the same." A sad smile passed over her face. "Unfortunately, those moments are also among the rarest."

They hugged, and Emmanua raised an arm toward the gates.

"Go, our friends. Safe travels. May you find what you seek, and may what you find be what you want."

Rucksack took Wander's hand, and together they left the city. Wander looked ahead, toward the future, toward the land beyond the road between the waves. But for just a moment, Wander also looked down, at the moment when one footstep passed over the green marble of the beautiful city—and the next, when yet again, both travelers stood on the ash and char of the Black Road. Wander sighed, and they continued on.

As they walked, Wander looked back briefly and saw that the gates of the city were still open.

"It's symbolic," said Rucksack. "They'll stay open until we're out o' sight. To show that they mean what they say."

"I have no doubt." Wander gave a sly grin.

"Now will you tell me?"

Wander nodded. "I asked Emmanua this morning over breakfast, while you were getting us more beer. She asked if there was anything they could do for us. I told her about Fiach, what she sought, and the danger she represented."

"But what can you expect Emmanua to do? This is a place o' peace, not o' military or fighting prowess."

"No," said Wander, "but it is a place of people who know the importance of walls and gates you can't get past. Tell me: If we hadn't been allowed inside the gates to begin with, how would you have gotten us in?"

Rucksack's brow furrowed. "To be honest, I don't know if I could have, much as I hate to admit it. Those gates and walls were well constructed, and the city is well watched and guarded."

"Then imagine the trouble Fiach will have."

"But there is slyness and deception to her."

"None of that will matter to the people of the city, Rucksack," replied Wander. "Emmanua felt she owed us a favor for deceiving us. She and the people of this city will do whatever it takes to honor their word."

"Which is?"

"They will bar the gates against Fiach. She will not be allowed entrance to or passage through the city. They won't imprison her, but neither will they allow her through. They'll turn her away."

Rucksack nodded. "Nicely done. Either she tries to climb the rock and come across that way, or she'll have to make her way back to Ireland, and catch the ferry across. All goes well, she'll arrive in England long after we have. We just may be able to make it to London and see about this chance o' getting you home before Fiach even touches foot to English soil."

Wander looked away.

"What is it?" Rucksack touched Wander's hand.

"Home," said Wander. "I chose to stay here."

"That was before you knew there was another possibility. If you could go home, you should at least get to look that opportunity in the face." Kindness and sadness swirled in Rucksack's eyes. "You owe it to yourself to have that opportunity. If there is a way, I will help you get there." He looked away, struggling with something, then managed to look Wander in the eye again. "Whatever you choose... I... I will support you."

They stopped, and Wander touched his face. "Thank you." They kissed, then continued on.

The city was long out of sight now. Nothing lay before them or behind them but the road.

"We'll make the most o' the time we have," said Rucksack. "Ultimately, that's all anyone can do."

And they did. Crossing the Black Road, they passed in joy and peace along the impossible road that lay between the waves.

Eventually the road began to slope upward. From the road between the waves, the seabed gave way to English soil—or rather, sand. Wander and Rucksack walked calmly into a new country, until they passed through a small village and saw smoke billowing from an inn.

Then they ran. Toward the flames. To do what they could.

37

FIRE

Smoke turned the sky gray and blotted out the sun as the long, narrow two-story building burned. Rucksack and Wander arrived at a crowd of people standing and staring.

Rucksack scanned the crowd and found a woman resembling an innkeeper: tidy and utilitarian, with a side of assessing every face to see who might try to sneak out before paying their bill.

"Everyone is out," the innkeeper said. "Staff, guests. I counted them myself." Then her face darkened, and she looked back at the flames. "Except one."

Wander started running, barely hearing the innkeeper say that the last person was on the second floor, at the very back of the building. Rucksack soon caught up, and he grabbed Wander's arm.

"What the hell do you think you're doing?" asked Rucksack.

"We have to help him," replied Wander. "That's what you do."

"What I do," said Rucksack. "But you aren't like me."

"Where you go, I go." Wander met and held Rucksack's gaze. "And right now we're wasting time." Wander shrugged off Rucksack's grip and ran into the burning building. He followed close behind.

Despite the hot air ripping at skin and lungs, Wander and

Rucksack pressed through the smoke and flames. They had entered the building near a rear staircase, and they dashed up it, avoiding the flames eating through the walls.

"We don't have much time!" yelled Rucksack.

"Do we ever?"

"You know what I mean. This whole place could go down any minute."

"Then let's not waste a second."

At the top of the stairs, flames ripped up the wall and onto the ceiling. Little bits of fire rained down, singing Wander, but Wander ran through the flames, looking left and right.

Last door on the right. Wander reached for it—but Rucksack knocked the hand away.

"It'll burn you." He grabbed and turned the doorknob. His glove smoked, but if he felt any of the pain searing into his left hand, his face betrayed nothing.

The door opened. On the far side of the room, air billowed in through a large glass door that opened on to a balcony. Behind them, the fresh fuel made the flames leap and grow. Wander shoved Rucksack into the room and dived after him. Where they had been standing moments ago, flames popped and snapped.

Wander slammed the door. "That'll buy us a little time."

The room had been simple but richly appointed. On a wooden desk on the wall to their right, documents smoldered, and a little book lay open. Nearby, a man lay unconscious on the floor.

The flames had only just begun eating through the walls, but the fire in the roof had caused a timber to fall. Most likely the man had been trying to get out of the room and the timber had hit him, both pinning him to the floor and knocking him out. But why was the door already open?

The man's skin was deep nut-brown and lustrous, despite the dust and ash settling on his bald head and on his bare face, like a young man's. He wore an orange suit jacket and an orange tie, and on his limp hands he wore white gloves.

"Quite the fashion statement, this one," said Wander. "Guy looks like a flame."

"Much as I appreciate your smart-arse banter," said Rucksack, "how about you put that breath into helping me move this damn beam. Feckin English oak must weigh more than half the inn."

Around them, the air from the open balcony door was making the flames in the room grow. The air became stiflingly hot, the air smokier and smokier. Despite a constant cough, Wander kept hold of the timber, helping Rucksack as he tried to lift and pivot it off the unconscious man.

They heaved. "Again!" shouted Rucksack. Around them, the walls groaned and crackled. Flames began popping out of the floor. "Hurry!" he said. "Floor's about to cave in. If it does, we are all going to burn."

"If you can survive The Blast"—Wander coughed—"surely you can manage this."

"It's not me I'm worried about. Now shift this damn thing!"

They pushed and turned and heaved, but the timber didn't move. Horrible cracking sounds blasted from the floor like gunshots. The air was so thick with smoke now. Wander kept coughing, but with each cough, with each breath, there was less real air to breathe in.

"One more, Wander," shouted Rucksack. "Come on, one more!"

The world swam in a boiling sea of orange flames. Wander took in whatever air was left in the room, then pushed.

The timber rocked off the man, and Rucksack knocked it away. He swooped down and picked up the unconscious man, flinging him over his right shoulder. "Get out o' here!"

Wander started to move, then turned to the desk near where the man had been lying. The way he had been lying there—the open balcony door—he must have opened the door to leave, then realized the book was still here and came back for it. Wander picked up the little book that lay open there and read some of the lines. With each word, color left Wander's face. "Rucksack."

"What?"

"The man. He's—"

With a crack, more flames swirled and another timber fell out of the ceiling. As it fell, a corner smacked Wander in the head. Wander fell hard, head smacking on the floor.

"Wander!"

The floor cracked and began to dimple in the middle.

Rucksack leaped to where Wander lay unconscious. He breathed in, as if daring the smoke to do anything other than nourish him. Then, for just one moment, the air filled not with the sounds of burning and crackling, the sounds of crumbling and exploding, but with a sound like the roar of a tiger.

With the unconscious man on one shoulder, Rucksack swung Wander over the other.

The floor began to collapse. From the hole in the floor, flames from below reached through like tentacles.

Rucksack leaped across the hole in the floor, bounded off the burning floorboards on the other side, and bounced back into the air. Where he had stepped, the floor crumbled and more flames reached out, burning all they touched.

Rucksack leaped through the open door and onto the balcony. The fire followed him, furious at being denied more material to burn. Rucksack didn't look back. He kept moving, holding Wander and the man on his shoulders as he bounded across the small balcony, then onto its railing.

The flames licked toward Wander.

Rucksack jumped.

38

ORANGE

The world must have split. That would explain the dull roar in Wander's head. That would explain the buzzing everywhere, and the ache—oh, the damn, damn ache—that rang with every breath.

"Don't even think about sitting up yet." Rucksack gave Wander's hand a squeeze.

"How long have I been out?"

"Long enough to terrify me."

"I'm back now."

Rucksack said nothing.

Wander sat up anyway. The pain roared fiercer now, but Wander ignored it. "Is everyone okay?"

Rucksack nodded. "The fire is mostly out. Whole damn building pretty much collapsed as soon as I leaped off the balcony."

"How did you do that?"

"What? Land safely?"

"Yes."

He shrugged. "It was easier when I could fly. We'll see if that part ever comes back. At least the falling part is still as easy as drinking a pint."

"Are you hurt?"

"Rolled my ankle a little. Some scrapes and mild burns."

"Nothing you haven't already healed from."

He said nothing.

"What is it, Rucksack?"

"That beam..." Rucksack looked away.

"Yes, it conked me good, but it was just a graze." Wander touched the scratch that ran from temple to jaw. "It could've been worse."

"That's the thing," said Rucksack. "It so easily could've been worse. Instead o' me checking your breathing and keeping you warm while all this settled down, I might be putting you in a grave."

"Keeping me warm shouldn't be hard," said Wander, trying to smile and regretting it but trying again despite the smacked and scratched flesh, which was agonizing.

"I don't get it."

"There was a massive fire. You know. Flames. Roaring fire." Wander's voice trailed off. "Easy to stay warm... Okay, you're right, horrible time for a joke."

"You could've been killed. Nearly were."

"Like it or not, you needed help." Wander sat closer to him. Rucksack didn't move away, but he also didn't come any closer. "Could you have gotten that timber off him without me?"

"No."

"Even the hero of old needs help sometimes. And I'm here. I'll help."

"You're here for now," said Rucksack.

"About that," Wander started to say, but then Rucksack jumped up. "What is it?" Wander tried to look around but couldn't see what he was seeing. Suddenly Wander felt really tired. The pain was harder now.

"Stop trying to do so much," said Rucksack.

"It's a scratch," said Wander. "I'll be okay. I'm just banged up."

"Not what I mean," said Rucksack. "Now hang on."

"Just a damn minute," Wander started to say, but Rucksack was already standing and moving, his bulk concealing his speed—and to all but Wander, his agitation.

The innkeeper came over to Rucksack. Behind her was the man in orange, who raised a hand toward Rucksack. Ash had grayed the glove, but Wander could still see the white. Even after the fire and all the dinginess, there was still a shininess to the fabric.

"Sir," said the innkeeper. "This is Mr. Deep."

"Thank you," said the man in orange, his voice hoarse from the smoke. His face, bald head, and clothes were all singed. "If it wasn't for you and your friend, I wouldn't have made it."

"It was the right thing that needed doing," replied Rucksack. The men shook hands, and Rucksack clasped his left black glove over the man's white glove.

"There was a book," said the man. "Did you happen to see it?"

Rucksack shrugged. "I'm sorry," he said. "But we were only able to save you."

The man sighed, disappointed but shrugging it off as best he could. "I wish to repay you," he said. "I know full well that you and your friend could have perished too."

"Pay it forward," said Rucksack. "That's all I need. Show the same mercy and kindness to someone someday who needs it."

The men stared each other in the eye.

"If you'll excuse me," said Rucksack, "I need to tend to my friend. I'll pass along your thanks."

The man in orange stood silent for a moment, then walked away, realizing the dismissal. Wander thought an orange gleam, like a flame, swung across the man's eyes, as if he felt slighted and angered—either from the dismissal, or from knowing that he was indebted to someone who had saved his life. That sort of account couldn't be easy to settle.

A horse-drawn carriage pulled up. The man in orange got inside and soon was gone.

"So that was him," said Wander, staring at Rucksack.

"That was him. That was who we risked our lives for."

"You sound displeased."

"Something about him," said Rucksack. "I don't necessarily get to choose who needs saving. I don't necessarily get to choose the good I do. I just do what needs to be done. But him... Something about him puts me off. Something in him, over him, like a shadow, as if somehow his true self were obscured. If I did have much o' a choice in the matter, there aren't many times where I would think twice about saving someone or leaving them to an unmeddled fate. But him... if I had time to think it over, or had to do it again..." Rucksack stared at the space where the man had been, where they had stared at each other as if seeing something familiar yet troubling. "I'm not saying I would have let him burn. But I would have had to think about it."

"We should get going," said Wander. "Get away from here before we draw attention. Besides, for all we know Fiach is getting close... maybe she's already in England."

"You're in no condition to go anywhere."

"You wandered for three days after The Blast, carrying your dead father over your shoulders."

"I'm different."

"You give me something to aspire to." Every muscle shook, but Wander fought upward, finally stood, then took a shaky step forward.

"What is it, Wander?"

"What do you mean?"

"You just seem in a hurry," said Rucksack.

Wander shrugged. It hurt.

Rucksack looked into Wander's eyes. "What were you looking at?"

"Huh?"

"Before the timber hit you. On the desk. Something got your attention. What was it?"

Wander's eyes widened. "Oh god."

"What is it?"

It came back now. The page, singed but clear. The book.

"It was him."

"Who was who?"

"Him. The man we saved. I read what he had written... Rucksack... the man we saved... everything in there was about us, and about Fiach. It's him. He's the Guru. He's the shadow."

Rucksack went pale. Then grinned. "At least the bastard owes me one for saving his life. And he'll still be wanting this."

Rucksack reached under the back of his shirt and pulled out the book. "You thought it was so important, you didn't drop it even after the timber dropped you. I figured I'd better hang on to it."

Wander smiled. "So it wasn't a terrible idea after all."

"No, it was a terrible idea," said Rucksack. "Luckily, sometimes good things can come from terrible ideas."

Rucksack caught the innkeeper's eye, and she came back over.

"I can't thank you enough," she said.

Rucksack nodded. "What did you say that man's name was?"

"Mr. Deep? It's a curious name, I'll give you that," said the innkeeper. "Let's see, it was... Guru Deep. That's it. Guru Deep."

Maybe it was something in Rucksack's eyes, or maybe someone had called over, but the innkeeper quickly moved on.

Rucksack reached back and unhooked the loops from the sword scabbards. "Let's get a move on, Wander, if you're okay to go. Should this Guru Deep realize who we are, I'd rather not be around."

They returned to the Black Road, sneaking away while

everyone else was busy putting out the last of the fire or tending to the wounded. Wander thought about how legends began, and realized this was part of it: When facts vanish, legends fill the void.

"We're going to be a story told down at the pub tonight, aren't we?"

Rucksack snorted. "What makes you say that?"

"Two people turn up when things are at their worst. They plunge into a burning building, no thought of anything other than how they can help. They save a man's life, just as the building comes down. One is hurt. There is a miraculous escape. Then, just at the moment of triumph and calm, they vanish." Wander nodded. "Yup, sounds like the stuff of legend to me."

Rucksack grinned, but it seemed that he had resisted it at first. "Wouldn't be the first time I've heard something o' the sort, no."

"What's going on?"

"You accepted being in this world," replied Rucksack, "but if you can leave..."

"I don't have to."

"And do what?"

"Stay. With you. Wander with you. We could be together. I can help you. This world... This world wasn't my home. But more and more it feels that wherever you are, that is somewhere I can call home."

"Things were always simple for me," said Rucksack. "That's the trade-off. Solitude has its loneliness, but simplicity compensates. You... are making things more complicated."

"Why? Because you have to worry about me when things get difficult?"

"That's part o' it."

Rucksack stared deep into Wander's eyes.

"I'll make a deal with you," said Wander. "We'll get to London, find this Jade person, and see if Emmanua was right that there might be a way for me to go back to my world. If there is, then I'll stand at that crossroads and decide. I'll stare into the world of my home, and into your eyes, and then I'll make my choice. But if I choose to stay here with you instead of going back to where I'm from, then we stick together for as long as we both want to. Fair?"

Rucksack kissed Wander.

"Fair," he replied.

They walked through the night, eventually stopping awhile to sleep.

Then, two days later, and with Wander healing well, they came to the edge of the city.

It had burned to nothing and taken an empire with it. The cries of thousands had faded into nothing. The very ground was charred blacker than the night sky.

Wander took Rucksack's hand. They paused and looked at the city that had burned—and that had risen from the ashes.

London.

39

ASHES

The city center was so much smaller than the London Wander knew, yet also brighter and more colorful. This wasn't the London of neutral sandstones and granites that Wander had seen. This London was bright and bold, with reds and oranges, blues and greens calling out to the world.

The people around them were also brightly dressed. Purples and yellows, greens and pinks. Here and there Wander saw the occasional neutral color, but mostly London's morning streets teemed with colors like a field of wildflowers.

"I don't understand," said Wander. "It's like I'm not in London."

Rucksack chuckled. "You're not in your London."

"My London has known its share of war and destruction too. But it's not like this."

"Awen told me The Blast made the world a more colorful place. How she explained it to me is that people gained this new love o' life. And that here, in London, it brought out a new vibrancy in people." Above them, a slate-gray sky pressed down on the city. "Besides," said Rucksack, "it's good to see Londoners realize their fashion doesn't have to match the dreary sky."

Wander cocked an eyebrow at him. "Says a man dressed all in black."

"When the day comes, I'll look different," replied Rucksack. "For now, I need to remember the char, the loss, the fire, the brutality. As long as I am making up for my mistakes in causing The Blast, I'll wear this black. It is my grief and my guilt. For now it is what I must show the world."

Wander kissed his cheek. "Then I long for the day when you know that you have paid the price you set on yourself."

They continued through London, north of the Thames River, until they came to the edge of a plaza.

Rucksack's face turned grim, and his mouth was a thin line. "Awen said this would be here," he said, "but it's still hard to face it."

"We'll cross together," said Wander. "I'm here."

The Square of Ashes was a flat black expanse, a memorial to the burning of London in The Blast. Awen had said it opened three days before Rucksack woke and before Wander arrived—exactly one hundred years after The Blast. Already people from all over the world had been coming to the Square, answering a call to remembrance, sharing their grief and their stories.

The black stone, Awen had told them, had been made with some of the ash and char that had been left of London. In each corner of the Square, round gray stone rose to a tall black column.

Atop each column, glimmering orange and red even in the dim cloudy light, a bright phoenix took flight.

They slowly walked across the Square. "Rucksack?" said Wander. "Are you okay?"

He said nothing at first. "I'm seeing all these people who are here because o' me," he said at last, his voice tight yet quavering. "How many o' them lost families, ancestors, in The Blast? How many o' them lost homes and farms and businesses, lost... lost everything?"

Wander sat him down on a stone bench. Rucksack's breath caught and hitched.

"Yes," said Wander. "They lost. Everyone loses something in this life. Rarely do we have any control or say. People make mistakes. Horrible things happen. What we lose matters—but so does what we use that loss to gain." Wander stretched out an arm. "Look at the people here, Rucksack. Some of them weep. But they are here, young and old. Children are with families, grandparents. Learning. Understanding."

"All this happened because I failed to stop The Blast," said Rucksack.

"And if you had stopped The Blast, then something else would have happened," replied Wander. "Hero though you are, that never meant you prevented every bad thing from happening in the world. If this place wasn't here commemorating The Blast, who knows, it would probably still be here, just in honor of some damn battle or something." Wander leaned down and looked him deep in the eyes. "No one can prevent life from knowing suffering, but you can show the world what suffering truly is."

"And what's that?"

"Suffering is an ingredient, not the totality of all things," said Wander. "Suffering can be transformed into something greater, something that transcends loss and pain. Suffering is what you turn it into, and you can turn it into kindness. Kindness is the child of love and suffering." Wander squeezed his hand. "The question is—my love, my friend—what are you going to do with your suffering?"

Tears coursed down Rucksack's face. "When we stood in Galway... where it all had happened... I lived it all again. It was like dying again. The world on fire. How this place suffered."

"And now they have remade London. The people came back," said Wander. "They defied The Blast. They defied the Black Road. They turned it into something else, moving char and ash until they had a city again. Their city. Because while The Blast and all that suffering was part of them, it was not the whole of them."

Rucksack nodded. They stood and stared at the people in the Square. Wander took Rucksack's hand and started walking.

"You can see it," said Wander. "That acknowledgement. There is suffering, death, grief. It's etched into every black stone." Wander smiled. "But there is so much more."

As they walked toward the center of the Square of Ashes, the stone lightened from darkness to a luminescent pearly gray.

"Until," said Wander, "we come to this."

At the very center, a small circular pool rose to their knees. The pool was made of a brilliant white stone, as if constructed of moonlight. In the pool, calm water shimmered.

"The Moon of Hope," they heard someone say.

"It's not what was destroyed," said Wander quietly. "It's what you do with the ashes."

Rucksack and Wander gazed at the pool, and at the people around them. Despite the darkness and sadness of the Square, there was a hope, a tinge of optimism.

"You can feel it," said Wander. "The people here. A determination. That when the world suffers, they will find a way to make it better."

A small grin came to Rucksack. "That sounds like something a hero should be doing."

Wander shrugged. "I thought you were supposed to care less about being the hero, and more about helping others find the hero in themselves."

"That's a tall order," said Rucksack.

Wander kissed his cheek. "You've done a damn fine job on me so far."

Some quiet time passed, while they looked at the Moon of Hope, at the Square of Ashes, at the people, at the brightly colored city surrounding them.

Then, when the time was right, Wander and Rucksack nodded at each other and stepped back from the Moon of Hope.

"So," said Wander, "where's this pub?"

40

THE END

"Word is," said Rucksack, "the Mirror & Phoenix opened three days after the Square o' Ashes."

"Three days," said Wander, staring at the bold black and brilliant red of the exterior.

Rucksack nodded. "The day you arrived and I woke up."

Wander grinned. "Will that get us a discount?"

Rucksack laughed. "I'm glad you're in good spirits."

"What do you mean?"

"Your way is close, Wander," said Rucksack. "Are you ready?"

Wander looked at Rucksack and nodded. Rucksack opened the door.

The pub's wooden tables were mostly empty, as were the booths and snugs lining the perimeter. Large plate-glass windows let in daylight, and also let people inside the pub see the Square of Ashes.

Behind the bar, a woman wore a white button-down shirt, black pants, and a blue bow tie. Her dark skin glowed in the lights of the bar.

"Welcome," said the bartender as Rucksack and Wander sat at the bar.

"Two pints o' GPS," said Rucksack.

"Of course."

The bartender walked off down the bar to pour the pints, the tight braids of her long black hair spilling down her shirt.

"Do you think that's her?" whispered Wander. "Is that Jade London, or is this the weird part of the quest where we're supposed to look for some bizarre, obscure clue?"

A few minutes later, the bartender came back with two brimming pints of stout. She set coasters on the bar. "For you, Rucksack," she said, "and for you, Wander."

"Oh," said Wander. "That was easier than I expected."

"Emmanua sent word." The bartender smiled. "And descriptions—along with arrangements for your tab. You two make quite an impression on folks. You can call me Jade." She nodded at Rucksack. "Nice swords."

"People typically can't see those," he replied. "Makes it easier to walk around in public."

Jade grinned. "I'm not typical people. Seeing the truth is part of a bartender's job—especially when someone is trying to conceal the truth."

"Sounds pretty heavy and philosophically profound for a service job," said Wander.

Jade shrugged. "Makes it easy to know when someone will try to skip out on their bar tab."

"If Emmanua sent word," said Rucksack, "then you know why we're here."

"There is a way back." Jade's gaze was kind as it settled on Wander, but it was the type of kindness that comes before bad news. "The way you seek, though..." Jade looked away, then looked back at them. "It's not here in London. You came all this way, believing you might find answers here. I'm sorry. There is an answer, but it's that you have farther to go."

"How far?" said Rucksack. "Where do we need to go?"

Jade sighed. "That's the trouble. I don't know. My... employers... don't know either. Such things are not well known to us. The best we know is that sometimes portals open up between worlds. They're rare. But if Wander has come through one already, then it's possible that just by being in the right place, Wander could make a portal open. Unfortunately, I don't know where that would be."

Customers came in. "Excuse me," said Jade.

Rucksack and Wander drank. "I'm sorry," said Rucksack. "We've come all this way. We'll figure out where to go. Together."

Wander's eyes widened. Pulling the daypack open, Wander pulled out the painting from another world. The shadowed, indistinct figure stood on a blackened outcropping, high above the sea. From below the edge of the high cliff, a soft glow seemed to shine upward.

Jade came over. "What is that?"

"Something I was given... back in my own world." Wander set it on the bar for Jade and Rucksack. "The person who made it—Paithoon, my Thai madwoman dream guide—said it was something she had seen in a dream, and she was sure the figure was me."

"Do you know this place, Jade?" said Rucksack. He looked from the painting to Wander. Fears and questions swirled in his gaze.

Jade nodded. "It's exactly where I would look for your portal: the end of the road. It's all the way at the southeastern tip of England. It's at the edge of the land, where the Black Road ends —at the Black Cliffs of Dover."

PART IV

41

ANSWER

D ay dawned over the end of the world.

Following the Black Road again, Rucksack and Wander had made the trek from London to just outside Dover in two days. At every turn, every strange sound from out of nowhere, they looked over their shoulders, certain that Fiach was behind them.

"Our luck can't hold forever," said Wander.

"We just need it to hold long enough," replied Rucksack. "We'll be at the Black Cliffs soon. Once we're there, you'll make your choice. One way or another, Fiach will not be able to get you."

"What if I decide to stay?"

Rucksack reached back and unhooked the little cords that secured the swords to their scabbards. "I'll make sure that Fiach will not be a threat to you anymore," he said. "Or to anyone else her precious damn guru might dare to send after us."

"You didn't know," said Wander. "Not any more than I did. Even if you had, I would have made the same choice."

"Time will tell," said Rucksack, a raspy darkness in his voice. "That decision could come to rule the destiny o' many."

Wander shrugged. "In the end, doesn't every choice?"

They continued down their dark path, going over little hills and rises, each step bringing them closer to the end of the road. Wander tried to imagine what it would be like. After so long on the darkness, so long seeing little but black, it was hard to believe that the road had an end. That the black would give way to the blue of the ocean. No more impossible roads. Just the waves and the sky.

Wander wondered what the portal would look like. Jade could not say exactly how it would happen, but her hypothesis was that Wander's presence would be like a key turning in a lock. Beyond, the world of home.

But here was the world Wander was getting to know. A world with so many questions to answer. What had happened to Awen? Was the guru's ancestor the figure whose shadow Rucksack had seen above the dia ubh, right before The Blast happened? What had the guru's ancestor done to cause The Blast?

Above all, Wander tried not to think about Rucksack and whatever was happening between them. The ease Wander felt next to him was something unknown. A peace, a calm, yet also an excitement, a sense of completion. For all that Wander had seen of the world, life had never stretched so far with possibility as it had in the weeks since Wander had first bumped into Faddah Rucksack in the hills of Connemara.

For now, Wander held Rucksack's hand and they walked down the Black Road. Toward the end.

Another rise, and there it was at last. Wander could just begin to see the end of the world. The Black Road was taking them straight toward it.

Then, seeing a small building, Rucksack pulled Wander off the Black Road.

"What are we doing?" asked Wander.

"I want to show you something first," said Rucksack.

"What?"

"The answer to a question that's been bothering you. All these years. All this time. It's the same question that vexes every person in every world at every time at every point in their lives."

"And what question is that?"

Rucksack smiled. "What is the meaning o' life?"

42

—————

THE CHALKBOARD

"Why are we looking for the meaning of life in an abandoned schoolhouse?" asked Wander. "Last I checked, schools had more to do with obscuring the meaning of life than with lighting the way."

Rucksack laughed. "Fair point. But this one is a little different. Long time ago, I helped build the place. Didn't dare to hope that it was still here."

"What?"

"I was traveling through this region, helped some folks having a difficult time o' some things. Realized that what they needed was a way to help their children learn. So we built this place together. A little school, for boys and girls to better themselves and make a better place and future." He winked. "It also, I must confess, was a wonderfully convenient place to hide the meaning o' life."

"You needed to hide it?"

"Makes it easier to show people when they need showing." Rucksack beamed. "The fact that it's still here makes me glad things worked out this way."

Outside the dilapidated building, they stopped at the door.

"The thing about the meaning o' life is it's portable," said Rucksack. "It's valid wherever you go—even if you're going to a different world. This is no small thing for a wanderer, because that also makes the meaning o' life sometimes hard to live yet always easy to travel with."

"Where I come from," said Wander, "this stuff is usually hidden. In the halls of a university, or buried in some secret spot in an ancient cathedral. A cave high in the mountains. Maybe a monastery, or stone circles in Scotland or Ireland, or the pyramids of Egypt. And usually you'd be looking for some wizened old mystic in some far-off nowhere."

"Close enough," said Rucksack. "Though I'm glad I'm not all that wrinkled. At my age, I'd be nothing but folds."

The door creaked as Rucksack opened it. They stepped into a little foyer. The walls on either side still had the hooks where children would have hung their coats. Beyond that, Rucksack and Wander went down a dim, low, narrow hallway, which opened up into a single large classroom. Little dusty desks filled two-thirds of the room. Across from the doorway where Rucksack and Wander entered, at the opposite end of the room, stood a freestanding chalkboard on wheels.

"The meaning o' life is here," said Rucksack, "but be certain that you truly want to understand. There is no going back."

"Where is it?" asked Wander.

He nodded toward the chalkboard. "On the other side."

Wander went toward it and stopped just in front. "If I go around, that's it," said Wander. "I'll learn something amazing. Something life-changing. Will I gain what I hope to gain?"

Rucksack shrugged. "That's up to you."

Wander kept stepping toward the other side of the chalkboard, but stopped each time. "What if I can't accept the truth? What if I disagree? What if I can never live up to it?"

"A journey o' a thousand miles begins with a single step."

Rucksack quoted Lao Tzu with bombast, then added, gently, "But it ends with a single step too."

Wander stared at him.

"You've come so far," said Rucksack. "Where else do you think you could ever travel that would matter as much?"

Wander sighed, nodded—and walked around to see what was on the other side.

Rucksack smiled.

Wander gasped. "But it can't."

Rucksack chuckled. "You're smarter than that." He came to Wander's side and they looked together.

The chalkboard was empty.

"Was it erased?" asked Wander. "Who could've done such a thing?"

Rucksack picked up a piece of chalk. "You could write something, you know, if you think this isn't enough."

Wander thought about it. "I could write something. Maybe I had figured it out already, during all my wanderings." Then the understanding began to dawn. "No," said Wander. "It wasn't wiped clean. It was blank to begin with."

"Right in one. Though if you have something to add beyond that—"

"I already know what to say."

"Some go for the blank," Rucksack replied. "They say it's all empty. They treat it as a finality. Immutable and inarguable."

"Is that valid?"

"For them. They just always run into trouble when they oppose someone who filled the emptiness with something else."

"I can never *un*-understand, can I?"

Rucksack laid a gentle hand on Wander's shoulder. "Would you want to?"

Wander stepped away from the chalkboard. "I don't need to add anything. I did understand. Because the meaning of life is simple. Life has no meaning except for what we give, for what we decide, and for what we live. All is blank and empty, except for what we fill it with."

Rucksack smiled.

For a few minutes they stared at the chalkboard, then Wander walked out of the classroom, passing into the foyer. The sound of chalk on a chalkboard made Wander turn around and run back into the classroom.

Rucksack smiled as he read something on the chalkboard.

"Always," he said.

Then he erased it.

Wander ran to him. "What did you write?"

"Something for me," he said, a sadness in his eyes. "Something that I'll need to remember later."

"Then why did you erase it?"

"I didn't," replied Rucksack. "I swept the chalk from the board." He tapped his forehead, then his heart. "But I didn't erase it. It's right where it needs to be. Where I'll always keep it."

He kissed Wander on the forehead. Then they left the schoolhouse and went to the end of the world.

43

THE CHOICE

"Any sign?" asked Wander

"You'll be the one to tell me," said Rucksack. "Not the other way around."

"So for now we just wait?"

"Yes." Rucksack smiled. "But that doesn't sound so bad."

They stood next to each other and stared out across the English Channel. Beyond the black edge, the sea crashed three hundred and fifty feet below. Beyond the gray-blue sea was France. Beyond was the rest of the world. So similar to the world Wander had lived in, yet so different.

"My world is so broken," said Wander. "We've known horrible things, but it's like we don't learn from them, so we keep doing more horrible things. Do you think that this world may have become a better place because of The Blast?"

"No," said Rucksack. "The Blast told everyone that there was a tenuousness to things, a fragility. This world has become better because people decided they would take better care o' the world and better care o' each other." He looked at Wander. "What do you think you'll do?"

Wander shrugged. "I can't answer that yet. I need to see the portal. You can't choose a path until you're standing at the crossroads."

The late morning sky had cleared, and brilliant sunshine poured across the Black Cliffs of Dover. Looking down, Wander could see the light glinting on the char. As far as Wander could see in either direction, the blackness was total, same as Galway. The fires of The Blast had licked down the cliffs, spreading across the entire face and turning white to black. The place was a wasteland now. Wander thought back to all that had happened over the last few weeks. A different life in a different world. After so much had happened, after they had been through so much, Wander was standing at the edge of the quest.

The power of the Black Road was less here. Wander was grateful for that. They could see the sky and the sea clearly, and the warm brilliance of the sunlight shone down. There was no dulling or dimming of the world. Not here. Wander smiled, and a great peace followed. In the distance, between the sky and the sea, a white bird flew, swooping up, then down, then out of sight.

A laugh made them turn.

Fiach raised a pistol. "You will come to my master now."

Rucksack took a step. Fiach fired. The impact spun Rucksack around and sent him over the edge of the cliff.

Wander screamed. Over the cliff's edge, Rucksack was nowhere to be seen. Wander turned and screamed again—but this time, it was more like a roar.

"You're no warrior," said Fiach.

"Not usually," Wander replied. "But in your case I'll make an exception."

Fiach started to level the pistol again, but Wander ran fast. There was no thought or plan now, no sense of anything other than reaching Fiach and making her pay for Awen, pay for Rucksack.

"I'll shoot!" yelled Fiach.

Wander just smiled—and tackled Fiach.

The pistol clattered away as they rolled along the ground. Wander came up on top of Fiach and began punching her, fist after fist after fist. Blood spouted from Fiach's nose.

Wander swung another punch, but Fiach caught it and knocked Wander away. Wander's face scratched across the ground. Before Wander could recover, Fiach was on her feet. She kicked Wander hard in the ribs. Wander slammed to the ground and gasped for breath.

Fiach grabbed the pistol and raised it.

"You won't shoot me," said Wander. "Your precious master won't want that, you damn dog."

"No, he won't," said Fiach. She turned the pistol so she held it by the barrel, and smacked Wander in the face. Pain seared down Wander's cheekbone, and the world swam as Wander's head hit the ground. Fiach kicked and kicked. Wander realized there was no fighting back, no way to defeat this, no way to win.

The blows stopped. Wander lay on the ground, bleeding from a few places, and sore everywhere else.

"I understood it the moment I saw you," said Fiach. Rage distorted her face. "All your life you've done as you wished. Gone where you wanted. Lived a false freedom I have never known, and I'm glad not to have known it. You think I live in terror and control? I live in the liberation of knowing that my master is taking me to the ultimate freedom. Freedom from this life, from this dream. You are so blind. You think you are free. You are a fool. I've dealt with fools before, brought them to my master without feeling or passion. But for all I have done to help Guru Deep, I have never hated anyone as I have hated you."

Fiach raised the pistol and put her finger on the trigger.

Wander remembered the last hope remaining. "Your master wants me alive."

"He will be sad yet will understand when I explain your unavoidable death." Fiach squeezed the trigger.

Wander's eyes closed. The world exploded. A hot wind rushed past Wander's temple.

A gloved right hand was twisting Fiach's wrist, and she yelped. Rucksack tore the gun from her hand and threw it over the cliff, then flung her backwards. Fiach hit the ground hard, and she coughed to get her breath back. Rucksack drew one of his swords and pointed it toward Fiach. The sharp point glinted in the light.

Wander sat up, body screaming in agony, but determined to get off the ground.

"I must do what he says," said Fiach, slowly standing.

"Over on the opposite coast, Rucksack and I pulled a man from a burning inn," said Wander. "If it had been you, honestly, then I don't know if I would have saved you or gotten a bag of marshmallows and a stick."

Fiach's eyes widened. "An inn?" she said. "On the coast?"

"Yeah. Your precious Guru Deep," said Wander. "We didn't know it was him until later. But we saved his life."

Fiach took a step back. "You," she said. "You... He did not know. He was waiting for me to arrive on the ferry..."

"Yeah." Wander took a step forward. "So here's what I think: In exchange for saving your master's life, you owe me. Walk away. Never bother me again."

Confusion stormed over Fiach's face. "You... saved Guru Deep... But I cannot... He will never forgive me..."

"I wasn't finished," said Wander. "Give up the guru. He doesn't have to control you anymore. Go make your own life. Be free of him. Live the freedom that is your right. You've never known anything but his control. Get to know living under your own control instead."

Fiach shook her head. "He has been all I've known since I was a little girl."

"Then it's time to learn something else." Rucksack lowered the sword and extended his gloved left hand. "You're not really living; you're just surviving at his whim. You don't have to be this way, Fiach. Leave him behind. He is a shadow darkening the world, taking away its light. Don't let him take away yours. You are his prisoner, but you can free yourself. Come with me. Find a new way. Please."

Fiach stared at them, silent, and Wander could see the battle in the woman's eyes, between a new desire for freedom, and the fear of defiance. But what would win out?

"I have no destiny but what he gives me," said Fiach at last. She moved in a blur, knocking Wander down, and then Rucksack too. Fiach picked up his sword and plunged it toward Rucksack's heart.

44

———

LEAP

Fiach yelled—and stopped. The tip of the sword glinted in the sun as it hovered just over Rucksack's chest.

"I can't kill you," she said. "You saved Guru Deep. You're so confusing. You... him..."

She turned and dropped the sword. The point stuck in the ground. Fiach's eyes shone, and tears ran down her face.

"A different life," said Fiach. "For me? All that possibility?"

Wander stood and hobbled toward Rucksack, standing between him and the cliff's edge, which was just a few feet behind. "A different life," said Wander. "Please, just stop this."

Fiach looked up at Wander, and the tears burned away, replaced by a deep rage. "Guru Deep has ordered me to bring you to him," said Fiach, "but I hate you. Every time I look at you, I want to kill you. You and all your freedom. Wandering the world. Doing what you want. You have the life I never had, could never have. And now you say that I could have it too? You know nothing. You don't know what it is to have displeased him. But I... I..."

Fiach's eyes lost focus, then it came back. She stared at Wander. "I can't make the choice you want to make. Maybe he'll understand." Fiach ran toward Wander.

Rucksack stood, but he was too late.

Wander had nowhere to turn, or to run to, or dodge, and Fiach was so fast, so fast—

The hunter of souls glared at Wander with burning eyes—then she leaped.

Past Wander. Over the edge of the Black Cliffs, toward the rocks and waves below.

45

OPEN

The broken body lay still on the rocks below.

"Is she dead?" said Wander, shaking but trying to remain standing. "I know it probably sounds stupid to ask, but you know how things go. In a story you always think someone is dead, but then it turns out a flock of pigeons caught them on the way down, or they faked a broken neck, or it was their twin."

"That might do for stories," said Rucksack, "but even from here I can see that Fiach's neck is so twisted she could see Guru Deep's whip at her back. She's dead."

Gradually, the waves of the changing tide pulled at Fiach. The body of the hunter of souls gently slid into the water and was gone.

Rucksack and Wander embraced.

"She could have made a different choice," said Wander at last. "But in the end she couldn't."

"She did, though," said Rucksack. "She could've killed me, but she didn't. She wanted to kill you. Your freedom, so opposite her slavery, made her hate you. She wanted to kill you, despite her master's orders."

"But she didn't," said Wander. "In the end, she made the only free choice she thought she could make." Wander sighed. "The guru is still out there, though. Because of us. We saved his life."

"That will be as it will be," said Rucksack. "Sooner or later, he'll have his time. I don't know who he is. Maybe he's long-lived and is the same person who caused The Blast. Maybe he is a descendant o' the one who did. I don't know yet. But the fact that he's alive... it'll work out, Wander. I don't know how. But I believe it will."

"She's not the only one with a choice to make," said Wander. "Now it's my turn to decide. Stay or go."

They stood there for a while, holding one another, saying nothing.

Then Wander looked around.

"What is it?" asked Rucksack.

"I don't know," said Wander. "It's... It's like something is tugging on me." They looked and looked, but saw nothing.

A hum filled the air.

"Wander?" asked Rucksack.

Wander's face went pale. "Before I fell into this world, I heard this same sound."

"Then why don't we see the portal anywhere?"

The sense of pulling continued. Wander's eyes widened.

Of course. It had to be.

Slowly, Wander turned.

And looked down.

About ten feet wide, the portal shimmered in the air with a soft glow—but it hung halfway down the cliffs.

Rucksack took a step back. "You see it," he said. "And you see me."

"But it's not exactly something I can skip through," said Wander.

"Doesn't matter." Rucksack tried to keep his voice even, but Wander could see the tension in his face, the tightness around his mouth. "The end of a quest is the beginning of a new choice—but first you have to choose. I can't choose for you. You've known that all along. You have to do what you believe is right. No matter what."

Wander stared out at the English Channel. It looked just like the painting.

Wander looked down at the portal. And saw it.

Wander looked back at Rucksack. And saw it there too.

Home.

46

PREY

The portal led to everything Wander had ever known.

A world to roam.

People to meet and then leave.

A world torn by violence and unrest, distrust and fear.

A world of loneliness and of aloneness.

Wander looked at Rucksack again.

Yet here was a new world. A world of possibilities, with limits as yet unknown, a world where Wander had no past, only a present and a future. Wander smiled and Rucksack smiled back. And Wander understood.

"What is it?" asked Rucksack.

"I see it all," said Wander. "I have nothing there to go back to. Not really. No family. No friends. Just more places where I could get stamps for my passport. I'm good at alone but not always good at lonely, and there's a lot of lonely waiting for me over there." Wander walked over to Rucksack and kissed him. "But here," said Wander. "Here I have everything, because I have you. Together we can have a great love, a great future, a great present. Here I can be home, because home is wherever you are. Whatever you need to do, I can help you. The shadow. Finding out what happened to Awen. Your destiny. All of it. Whatever comes, whatever we must do, I can be there and be part of it."

"So you've chosen?" asked Rucksack.

Wander nodded. And kissed him again.

When they came apart, tears streaked down Wander's face. "Wander?"

Turning again, Wander looked toward France. Despite the blue sky, a shadow lay over the eastern edge of the world, as if a gathering storm were preparing to blow the world down.

"I understand," said Wander, turning back and trailing a hand down Rucksack's face. "If I choose to stay. Fiach is dead, but the danger isn't gone. It's only just begun. Shantermon showed us that. Fiach showed us that. The shadow is getting stronger, and Guru Deep won't stop. I'm prey. Not a traveler. Not your love. Prey. As long as I'm in this world, he'll know. Guru Deep will pursue me, hunt me, until he has me. He'll kill or hurt whomever he must to get to me. He'll kill you."

"I can take care o' myself. I can protect—"

"Not always. We both know it," said Wander. "In the fire... I nearly died. I can be a distraction. I will be a distraction. A weakness. You can't have those right now. I will always be hunted, threatened. My Rucksack, my dear Rucksack, I want to be with you."

"I want you to stay. I don't care."

"I will always hold you back. I will always be a risk that you cannot take. I can't have that. I couldn't live with it. I love you, Faddah Rucksack, and I love you far too much to hinder you."

Rucksack stroked Wander's hair. "What if I went with you?"

"You know as well as I do that's not an option. You have so much to do. You have so much to set right. This is your world, where you belong. It needs you. Besides, what you do here may very well save me in my world."

"I might need help."

Wander laughed. "Oh, you definitely need help. You'll find it, though. You love this world, and this world will show you how much it loves you too." Wander kissed him. "Take it from one who knows."

"I see the wisdom in what you say," said Rucksack, "but I don't want to accept it."

"I was told once that when the time was right, I would face a choice," replied Wander. "When I did, the entire world, all of life, maybe even the entire universe, would rest on that decision. I've wondered when that moment and I would find each other. That crossroads is here, my love. That time is now. I have to make this choice, Rucksack. There are other ways, yes, but none of them are right. I feel it. I know it. I've seen the chalkboard. I know my meaning of life."

Tears streaked down Rucksack's face as he set his hand over Wander's heart. "I understand."

"I know."

"That doesn't make it hurt any less."

"Sometimes," said Wander, "the pain of the truth is the only way to know how real something is."

They kissed, one final time, one kiss for a lifetime, for a future that could not be, for the future that had to be.

Then, at last, Wander gave Rucksack's hand one final squeeze and went to the edge of the cliff. Staring down at the portal, Wander's eyes closed, then opened. Wander's legs tensed—

"Wait."

"Rucksack, don't make this harder than it already is."

"It's not that. I want you to have something before you go."

As he came over, he took the glove off his right hand and held it out.

"It's small enough to carry in a backpack, and it will always be a bit o' me, a bit o' this world that you can keep with you over there," said Rucksack. "A souvenir. A memento. Keep it."

Wander nodded and took the glove.

"This world is home for you too, and it will always be waiting for you. I promise on all that I have been, am, and will be," added Rucksack. "If ever you come back here, find a way to get this glove to me. There's not another like it in the world. I'll know it the moment I see it. Wherever you are, I will find you. Whatever you need, I will give it."

"I have a gift for you too." Wander opened the daypack and gave him the painting.

Rucksack smiled, and Wander said, "One more thing." Leaning forward, Wander whispered one word into Rucksack's ear.

Pulling away, Wander added, "I haven't used my birth name in years, but it's still part of me. Now at least someone in this world knows it too."

"I'll treasure it," said Rucksack. "Always." He stepped back.

Wander looked at him one last time.

Then, Wander turned and stared down at the portal, wincing a little at its glow, and drew in a last breath.

Miss the portal, die on the rocks. It had to be perfect. Wander focused, trying to ignore Rucksack standing there, just a few feet away, raising his gloved left hand, his fingers outstretched.

Wander stepped.

47

GLEAM

As the world rushed by, Wander turned. The edge was farther and farther away. Wander looked instead at the black cliff. So dark. Burned by the calamity. Forever darkened by The Blast.

Then, as Wander fell, hoping the aim was true, it became visible, shining there like a solitary star in a lonely black sky.

A gleam in the dark.

On the blackened cliff, a speck of white.

Wander smiled.

Eyes closed, Wander kept seeing that little bit of white.

Then the fall was done.

PART V

48

NEW ROAD

The schoolhouse door creaked open, then clacked shut.

For the first time in a long time, Faddah Rucksack opened his eyes. From where he sat, legs crossed, next to the chalkboard, the hallway and foyer looked empty. But that sound hadn't been the wind or an animal. He would have caught an animal's scent. Mere wind wouldn't have roused him.

Thin daylight came in through the east window, enough both to cast gloom and to bring the promise of illumination to the empty classroom. The hallway and the foyer, though, were without windows. Darkness still lay thick over them.

Rucksack's eyes widened and he called out, "Wander?"

The door closed. Softly. As if someone hadn't wanted to be noticed.

"Or just someone who didn't want to disturb you any more than they already had," said a familiar voice.

Rucksack stood. "How can it be?"

Outside, the sun rose higher, more daylight came into the room, and so did the Awen of Ireland.

Her robes were a brilliant white, as if made of moonlight. So was her new traveling staff, which she leaned against the wall.

Awen touched his face. "How long have you been here?"

"It's been thirty-three days since Wander left this world," said Rucksack. "Your turn. How did you survive Fiach?"

Awen shrugged. "She put up one hell of a fight. I just had more in me. Finally I got the best of her. Actually had her locked up for a bit, in an old circus wagon I found. I'd gone part of the way back toward central Ireland when she woke up. Being in the wagon... it just about drove her mad. She ranted that she wouldn't stay there, hadn't done anything wrong, hadn't disobeyed. She broke free and I lost track of her. I followed, hoping to catch you. It's hard being out of Ireland, but worth it to find you at last, my friend."

"Fiach suffered greatly," said Rucksack. "In the end, I had pity for her. But also hope."

"Because she deserved it?"

Rucksack shrugged. "Because I have to have that hope. The Blast happened because o' my failure, Awen. I'll always have to live with that. I'll always face condemnation for that. And fair enough. I have to believe that someone like Fiach could come to find goodness despite failings and horrible happenings—because that's the only way that I have a chance too."

Rucksack and Awen told each other more of what had happened since they had separated, until Rucksack reached the moment where Wander had stepped off the cliff. "By the time I got to the edge, there was no sign o' Wander, and the portal had closed." His voice broke. "The portal or the rocks. I'll never know."

"From a cave to a classroom," said Awen. "At least you're up and about sooner this time. Whatever grief you feel, Wander made the right choice."

"I've lost so much," said Rucksack. "All this time, all these years, I never knew love like that. Till Wander. It was new, and I don't know what would have happened down the road, but I had it, I knew it, and now I see why people make such a bother about it. Tis true and wonderful stuff."

"But it also cuts deep," said Awen. "It leaves you no defense except itself, yet it also becomes your greatest vulnerability. Some would say your greatest weakness."

"Ultimately that's why Wander chose to go," he said. "But it's not just for Wander that I grieved. Mum. Dad. The destiny I once knew I was moving toward. All the things I've done since I woke, and I still don't know where I'm going."

Awen shrugged. "Never stopped you before."

"Maybe it's time that changed."

"No," said Awen. "Maybe it's time you embraced it. All those years, you wanted to pursue that destiny, make it come true. But it didn't. Whatever happened to upend it and cause The Blast, happened." Awen stared at him. "Do you know why you woke up in the cave?"

"I've wondered if it's because, for the first time in a hundred years, I dreamed about The Blast," said Rucksack. "I spent a hundred years dreaming o' my first ten thousand. But never about The Blast. Until the day I woke up."

"You didn't wake up the day that you dreamed about The Blast," said Awen. "You woke up the day, the moment, that Wander arrived. When you were needed most."

Rucksack nodded. "Only I didn't realize it at first, but I needed Wander too."

"I'm glad you and Wander were there for each other."

"I wish there could have been more."

"But you loved what you had. You'll never stop appreciating and treasuring it." Awen touched his shoulder. "You have known the beginning of great love," she said. "You have even had a chance to grieve the loss of that love, but I'm afraid it's time to move on. It's time for you not to worry about knowing and simply put one foot in front of the other again. Go where the world takes you, where it needs you to be. You'll find your way; you just won't necessarily know which way you're going. Not till you get there anyway."

"You can't choose a path until you're standing at the cross-roads." Rucksack sighed. "I have to save the world again?"

"Destiny is what you choose to make of circumstance," said Awen. "You've always been good at showing that to others. Now it's time to live it for yourself. It's not about the saving. You are more than that. For all your years, your greatest moments have been not in battle or combat, but in change and transformation. You didn't see in me some warrior. You looked not for blood but for light. You found it, and you helped me bring it out of myself, till it became who I am."

"I am not just light, Awen. I am darkness as well. Blood and fire. You know that."

"Of course. But you have your own light too, Faddah Ruck-sack. The shadow, this Guru Deep, knows this. He fears you." Awen grinned. "He should. You found me because you needed to pass on the best of yourself, and what you passed on was light, guidance, and inspiration. Now I'm passing it back to you. You must inspire others. Help them find the heroes in themselves. The hero the world needs is the hero in every person."

"I'll continue," said Rucksack. "For the world. For Wander. For you. For all who died in The Blast."

"No," said Awen. "This is not a funeral quest. You will continue for all those who live, and all those who will live. All those who love and will love. As you have."

"What now then?"

"Learn all you can about Guru Deep," said Awen. "His shadow is growing, and we know very little. Find a way to bring your light to him, to shine in the darkness that is him—and then see what he does with it. Along the way, do all the good you can. Really, that's all we can ask of anyone. Even you."

They left the classroom together. Awen took up her staff, then in the foyer picked up her traveling cloak. She nodded at Rucksack's bare right hand. "You can replace that glove, you know."

Rucksack shook his head. "I gave it up for a reason. I'll think I'll leave it that way. To remind me."

Awen smiled, but as they turned to the door, the line of her mouth hardened again. "I'm not the only visitor you had, by the way." She pointed to something scrawled on the back of the door.

I found you.
I spared you.
We are even.
Till next time.

Rucksack pried up a floorboard. From the hollow inside, he picked up Guru Deep's book, which Wander had found in the burning inn. Rucksack grinned. "We'll see about that."

"Till next time," said Awen.

Outside, near the schoolhouse, the Black Road's eternal shadow scarred the world and mocked the high sun. Rucksack faced the dark gash, and saw it for the reminder that it was.

He stood still, eyes closed a moment as he felt the absence of all those lost—but also the anticipation of all those to be born. A cloud passed over the sun. For a moment, Rucksack's face was half in light, half in darkness. His black clothes were the roving shadow to the stillness of the Black Road's. The hilts of the crossed swords stuck out over his shoulders, and his bald brown head gleamed as the cloud passed and the daylight's full glory returned to shine brilliant sunlight on his smiling face.

With a nod, Awen and Rucksack turned away from the Black Road, and sought instead new paths to wander.

THANK YOU FOR READING

Please **tell people** about this story and **review it**.

Reviews are the best way readers discover great new books, and I would truly appreciate it. Even a couple of sentences is a big help.

Review Wander online:
anthonystclair.com/wander

BECOME A WANDERER

Early access to new stories... and much more
Back Anthony's fiction and non-fiction on Patreon

This story is made possible in part by my Wanderers, my patrons on Patreon. Wanderers back my work for as little as $1 per month. In return, they can get special rewards, exclusive access to me, e-books, signed books, early access to new stories, and more. You can be a patron too. Learn more and become a patron today:

patreon.com/anthonystclair

Free book
Get a free e-book of Anthony's acclaimed novel Forever the Road

When you join my free reading group via email, you'll get a free book, hear about new stories, events, and news, and more!

anthonystclair.com/freebook

ALSO BY ANTHONY ST. CLAIR

All Rucksack Universe titles are available in paperback and all e-book formats. Tap the title to learn more and buy from your favorite bookstore.

The Martini of Destiny

anthonystclair.com/martini

Home Sweet Road

anthonystclair.com/homesweetroad

Forever the Road

anthonystclair.com/forevertheroad

The Lotus and the Barley

anthonystclair.com/lotus

More stories & news

anthonystclair.com

To Jodie, Connor, and Aster.
You give this wanderer hope and home.

ACKNOWLEDGMENTS

Thank you to my patrons, who help make my stories possible by backing my work through Patreon. Patrons get special rewards, exclusive access to me, early access to new stories, and more. You can be a patron too. Learn more and become a patron today:

patreon.com/anthonystclair

Thank you to Bonnie Donaghy for cover design, and to Scott Alexander Jones for the spot-on copy editing, story advice, and proofreading. Any mistakes—especially when it comes to languages and cultures—are mine.

Above all, my thanks to my family. Connor and Aster, you inspire every story I write. Jodie, with you I am the man I'd always hoped to be.

www.anthonystclair.com

SPECIAL FEATURES

Go behind the scenes of the Rucksack Universe:

Check out the Special Features:

Become a patron for behind-the-scenes special access

Request an e-book autograph:

authorgraph.com/authors/anthonystclair

Reading Order
The Rucksack Universe is an ongoing, non-sequential series. Read
it in any order you like. If you want to know the order of release
or the order of the storylines, here are suggested reading orders:

Choose your reading itinerary:
anthonystclair.com/rucksackreadingorder

ABOUT THE AUTHOR

Anthony St. Clair creates compelling fiction and non-fiction for a curious world full of everyday discoveries, endeavors, and surprises. He is the author of the ongoing Rucksack Universe series; covers craft beer, food, business, and more for various publications; and is a copywriter and content manager for select clients. When not at his desk or in his kitchen in Oregon, Anthony is on an adventure with his wife, son, and daughter.

For more information:
anthonystclair.com

instagram.com/rucksackpress

twitter.com/anthonystclair

facebook.com/anthony.stclair.author

pinterest.com/anthonystclair

amazon.com/author/anthonystclair

goodreads.com/anthonystclair

youtube.com/anthonystclairauthor